I0557334

# GRAIL: TICK YOUR LIFE

# RIGHT, WITH PURPOSE

## The Anthology of Purpose

An initiative of

Mental Resilience Mastery

admin@mentalresiliencemastery.com

https://mentalresiliencemastery.com

An initiative of Mental Resilience Mastery © 2022

## Table of Contents

An initiative of Mental Resilience Mastery © 2022

An initiative of Mental Resilience Mastery © 2022

An initiative of Mental Resilience Mastery © 2022

# FOREWORD

It is my pleasure to write a foreword for the collective experiences authored by well-achieved life coaches in Grail- Tick Your Life Right, With Purpose.

The Book comes at a juncture in the history of humankind when humanity is struggling with an existential crisis. Never before have we all faced such a dire need for direction, purpose and meaning as in the post covid world. Indeed, we may not be out of the woods just yet.

At such a time, the authors have shared experiences of grace, persistence and purpose that lift the spirit and hand-hold humanity out of the darkness towards the light.

The personal struggles of the writers have motivated them to look at their experiences as life lessons which have shaped their personalities and lives post the "crucible moment". Experience is indeed a great teacher. But the one who learns from others' experiences is a great student.

An initiative of Mental Resilience Mastery © 2022

I wish the writers and their reader's great success. May this Book bring answers, meaning, purpose and drive to all.

Nishi Misra
Principal
Scindia Kanya Vidyalaya
Gwalior

An initiative of Mental Resilience Mastery © 2022

## Introduction TO CO-AUTHORS

| Name | Contribution |
| --- | --- |
| David Nair | Co-Author |
| Sonali Abhay Kothari | Co-Author |
| Alka S Oswal | Co-Author |
| Dr. Sumana Chakraborty | Co-Author |
| Nisha Subodh Chandak | Co-Author |
| Shikha Singh | Co-Author |
| Dr. Rajiv Agarwal | Co-Author |
| Supriya Pramod Rane | Co-Author |
| Jennifer Ann Bruk-Jackson | Co-Author |
| Monica Sodhi | Co-Author |
| Manju Kar | Co-Author |
| Pretiksha Diar | Co-Author |
| Nawaz Homi Marker | Co-Author |
| Dr. Alka Chadha | Co-Author |
| Jyoti Gidwani | Co-Author |
| Akanksha Kabra | Co-Author |
| Dr. Parvin Khan | Co-Author |
| Prabhunath Angad Pandey | Co-Author |
| Tushar Bhargava | Co-Author |
| Vaijayanti Bose | Co-Author |
| Bashiruddin Haroon | Co-Author |
| Amanpreet Kaur | Co-Author |
| Ansuya Uka Khoosal | Co-Author |
| Dr. Fauzia Shamshed | Co-Author |
| Rejina Eufemiano Francisco Barretto | Co-Author |
| Surbhi Pandey | Co-Author |
| Maila Venkateshwar Rao | Co-Author |
| Nutan Nakara | Co-Author |

An initiative of Mental Resilience Mastery © 2022

Kala Natrajan         Co-Author
Asha Bharti           Co-Author

An initiative of Mental Resilience Mastery © 2022

# STRENGTH

An initiative of Mental Resilience Mastery © 2022

## POSITIONAL CLARITY: RUDDER TO

## YOUR LIFE

*"Create a Mind-set, Heart-set, and Soul-set shift in one million minds, and their next generation, to stretch that little more in each of them, thereby contributing towards a better world for all of us and generations to come and leaving behind a Life of Significance."*
*-David Nair*

The start of my journey in transforming from a shy mamma's boy to a Corporate Strategist, Certified Practicing Accountant (CPA), Master NLP Practitioner, a Peak Performance Excellence Coach & Mentor to Corporate India, Keynote International Speaker and an Author, with a Definite Major Purpose (DMP) did not happen overnight; nor did it fall onto my lap in a silver platter.

Picture the image of a young, shy, frightened kid in a foreign land, thrown amidst a completely different tribe of youth – a group that was outgoing, boisterous and a go-getter. To top it off, living in a boarding secondary school for upward mobile kids who were on track to complete their enrolment. I had no previous exposure to living away from home, in a foreign land, with a culture of total foreign ideology, way of life, customs etc. Rather than empowering me, this put me into a downward spiral.

I was timid, backwards and fearful of interacting with people – I felt inadequate to talk, and I would feel this pain in the pits of my stomach. Even whilst in Malaysia, I would hide behind my mother's petticoat to greet friends and relatives visiting our home. That was how shy I was.

What would a teen in that frame of mind and state know about purpose? How significant would that be in his conversation? Absolutely Not. Purpose, unheard of, set a few materialistic goals such as completing my secondary and tertiary schooling, buying a car, saving up for travel, picking up enough courage to ask a girl out for a date, and saving up for a home. That's all that would be in my mind: A Life without Purpose's primary goal was directionless. This is akin to a chicken scratching the ground for worms. Primary simplistic Hand-to-mouth type of materialistic goals, instead of being an Eagle soaring in the sky.

Fast forward twenty years, how did such a person step up from being in that state and frame of mind to being able to have addressed an open-air stadium in India of 40000+ people? What caused him to burn his boat by leaving behind a high-flying career as the Asia Pacific Vice President of the third Largest Oil & and gas corporation bought a one-way ticket to head off to India. The mindset shift and transformation occurred through the guidance of coaches and mentors (fourteen to be precise) who helped me build myself and fill my internal cup to the point where it topped the brim for me to give. During this period, my Internal Bank account was gradually filled, with a prime focus on helping me crystallize my direction and my purpose in life. Hence the Birth of My Why, My Purpose. Yes, it was a priceless gift – the time, money and effort that was pumped into understanding and appreciating what A vital, Definite Major Purpose in Life will provide when built on a solid foundation of Faith, Decision and Commitment. The Certitude in how one moves through Faith, with the belief to cement the decision made with dogged determination and commitment. When you get into an activity or a project, you burn your boats and deep dive into that project wholeheartedly, as though your life depends on it. It is startling how the universe responds when you are internally and externally in sync. The universe observes this and acts accordingly in paying back multifold.

Armed with this belief and purpose, I stepped out in Faith and made the commitment and decision to plunge into driving my abovementioned purpose initially in India. I quit my Senior, well-paid job. My Dad thought I had lost my head and gone wild, while my nuclear family approved and accepted. I rode the wave to create that impact with people. Why? India gave my parents a perfect start in a foreign country Malaysia, where We had a good comfortable life. Hence, I wanted to give something back to my country, India and weaved my work around that payback.

I bought a one-way ticket and landed in India without a client; I knew nobody, as I had not been to India before that visit. With Faith, I sent out one hundred postal letters (not emails) to various organizations and community clubs to talk on a topic close to my heart "Design your Life" Hence I started my speaking career. Out of the one hundred letters, I received only one response from a Rotary Club in Chandigarh. I went to Chandigarh and spoke on my topic. It went across exceptionally well that I had received bookings in twenty-one cities in Pan India by the time I finished my talk. This is the birth of my client base of 50 + MNCs over the next three decades, I built a Training and Development.

Coaching & Mentoring Organization has helped empower over three hundred thousand people over the last three decades. We had the opportunity to impact people in ten other countries in Southeast Asia, the Middle East, Northern Europe UK, and South Africa.

Was this achieved by chance? A definite NO. When you work the fundamentals right with a Definite Major Purpose, the universe realigns and works the FLOW in your favour.

Some might call it LUCK; I ponder for a moment and say it is LUCK. This word is an acronym with a true meaning of Labour Under Correct Knowledge. I keep telling the thousands who attended my session that when you understand what success is and realize what it takes to build your foundation, YOU MAKE YOUR LUCK. This concentrated energy force, proficiency in fundament patterns, core values, and passion-filled purpose help you manifest your aspiration.

Is that A to B journey a straight line? No, in most cases. What do you do when it sways away? Simple: - With a strong Rudder, no matter how strong the wind blows, we adjust the sails windward, redirecting that sailing boat towards the set destination. That is why a strong Purpose is not essential; instead, Vital for our arrival at the set destination.

This purpose kept me making multiple trips back to India over the last three decades, despite the innumerable challenges of water, electricity, road system, bureaucracy and an endless list of other issues encountered. The challenges just faded to oblivion. I had a mentor who constantly reminded me by saying, "David, what are you focusing on? The Majors or the Minors of Life. The list of challenges encountered was minor compared to my prime purpose of impacting one million lives." Now when that is in your DNA, no Tsunami will uproot this Oak Tree

This purpose gets you to jump out of bed on a Monday morning. This purpose gets you to finish a 5-day training program despite having a high fever of 101degrees F. Its elements of passion reinforce the purpose, and it is layered one on top of the other until the set aspiration is manifested.

The above is a concise list of the reason for having a purpose; it does assist in your journey from point A to Point B. There are many other reasons that I have not cited, but I found the above substantive in helping me achieve what I have committed to date.

It would be remiss if I did not spend a few minutes on what we as a human race are pursuing in life. Is it manifesting material elements, contributory goals, or the one internal fire of contentment – true happiness- that we seek? As succinctly mentioned by the Dalai Lama–"The Purpose of our Life is to be Happy."

So, no matter how far you drive or sail to reach that point B in your destination, you have not fully succeeded if it lacks that element of contentment. So, what is this contentment? The happiness chemical that we need to balance within ourselves. It is commonly referred to as DOSE (Dopamine, Oxytocin, Serotonin, Endorphins) chemicals.

Briefly capsuled, my purpose was derived from these elements:

- **To be Happy** – where I did figure out my Core Values, Commandments and aligned my life around them
- **Fulfilling Potential** – I worked on myself to break through my roadblocks to achieve my outcomes
- **Make the change** – I had to overcome my fears and constantly work on transforming my mind, heart, health, and soul.
- Finally, find the balance – align my internal and external world by constantly measuring to ensure I am well centred.

An initiative of Mental Resilience Mastery © 2022

## David Nair:

https://linktr.ee/DavidNair

## UNKNOWN TO UNSTOPPABLE

My purpose in life is to be the light for those who want to upgrade their lives, be the best version of themselves, be who they indeed are, and create their own identity to design their dream life.

The most impactful day of my journey was the eve of 8th March 2019. I was facing the sky, spreading my arms with closed eyes on the seashore. My heart couldn't hold the flood of emotions and found its way to flow in the form of tears. However, at the same time, there was a heartfelt smile on my face. Waves of the sea witnessed that confluence of 2 different emotions, tears and a smile. I was so happy to send my deep gratitude to the Universe for making the day the most memorable day of my life. So, what happened that day?

I was in one of the elite 5-star hotels in Mumbai, the Sahara Star Hotel, in their colossal auditorium with more than 4000 audiences. The occasion was the breakthrough event of my Coach and Mentor, Mr Arfeen Khan, for which we all were super excited.

Finally, the moment had come for which I had been waiting for a long time. I got a chance, or I grabbed the opportunity, to say something on that stage, to share my experience.

I was very excited to tell the story of my transformation, the level of victory, the story of my journey, and how I achieved it. I started to walk towards the stage from the centre aisle, being very happy and a bit nervous too. When I began my talk, I momentarily felt that time had stopped. I shared how I had been reborn after coaching, how my relationships with my in-laws and relatives had changed, and how I discovered a new way to look at life.

I also shared a poem I wrote wherein, at my funeral, I saw how my life had unfurled.

Suddenly, a massive round of applause grabbed my attention. Every person stood up from their chair and expressed with their eyes that every word had touched their heart. I noticed that I was spotlighted on a massive screen behind me, flashing compliments for me like – "You are unstoppable", "You are Incredible", and many more. I was on cloud nine. I wanted to freeze this memorable moment forever. Afterwards, I went to a nearby beach with my buddies to celebrate this moment and express my gratitude to Universe.

When I returned to my room, my mind was in turmoil as it was referring to my memories and indicating that this was a dream only, not a possibility. I, too, tended to succumb to that thought for a moment before I bounced back.

A few years ago, I was a girl who could never be confident, could never express my feelings openly, could never take care of my happiness, and could never even stand for myself. Today, as I stood on that stage, I shared openly by being vulnerable. For someone, it may seem trivial, but for me, it was my achievement. That night, I visualised my whole life's journey in a flashback like a movie and realised how much I had grown.

So, what made me the person I am today? How did I come so far on this journey?

The secret which leads me to this discovery is the secret to our existence. The journey of finding a true sense of the meaning of my life will help you get answers to many of your questions that may pop up in your mind directly or indirectly. I am sure when you will reach the end of this chapter, either you will start to discover your purpose, or you will be even more committed to your goal.

I still remember how my life was in turmoil after marriage. My self-respect was depleted. The reason was simple. I could not respect myself, so why should the world? I was so bad that I lost myself and even forgot to smile.

It is like taking a bus with no destination when you don't know why you live. Wherever the wind blows, your life goes. My life became a roller coaster.

If someone said something to hurt me, I used to get offended and spent hours feeling bad, nervous and victimised. This emptiness and these compromises turned into anger & hate unconsciously. Whatever I was doing was from a space of lack of love, lack of fulfilment, lack of respect, and lack of happiness. I was burning my self-esteem and my care. It affected my personal and social life too.

Why did it happen? Why did I spend my precious, limited time on things which did not even matter? Why could I not channelise my energy to creating something meaningful or building my future? Why could I not develop resilience to bounce back?

Thank God my husband was the one who was always with me, no matter what. If not, I might have done something to harm myself.

So, what helped me to come out of that situation? How have I become the person I am today? This is the time when the "purpose" came into my life. I discovered my purpose; I wanted to create my identity.

The one thing that kept me going was my belief that there must be some meaning behind my existence. God could not create me as a human for no reason. My presence on earth matters. My life matters; my life has a purpose.

This faith gave me the courage to bounce back from any challenge. It gave me a reason to wake up every day. It made me feel lighter despite all the challenges. It gave me the ability to "Let Go". I knew that if I remained stuck on the question "Why Me", it would take me away from my purpose.

I did whatever I could to build myself. I conducted art classes and cake-making classes for women. I became a channel partner in Thumb Rule and helped people to discover their inborn potential with DMIT [Dermatoglyphic Multiple Intelligence Test]. I became an entrepreneur of Indian Handicrafts. I did so many things, which helped me generate a good profit. I got a good platform for my products in various IT companies. I helped underprivileged artisans to grow to earn. And slowly, my condition started to change. The behaviour of people around me changed.

In this whole journey, I realised that so many women are out there who are still struggling. I saw some of my relatives always compromising on their dreams. They were drifting in situations. They were completely unaware of the meaning of their lives. Though they were a mother, a daughter, a daughter-in-law or a wife, they could not create their identity. They were still struggling to make a joyful, meaningful life for themselves.

Did that mean they did not want to be happy? Didn't they deserve love, respect, or success? Did that mean they are worthless?

**No! Not at all.** Everyone wants and deserves to be happy, loved, and respected. However, they don't know how to be that person.

This whole reality blew my mind. My focus shifted from "ME" to "WE." I decided to change their conditions, to change their fact. I committed to being the light for them, guiding them to discover their dream life. Once I found my purpose in life, I never looked back.

My purpose honoured me with many hats, such as a Coach, a Speaker, an Author, an Influencer, an Entrepreneur, the Founder of "Mrs Unstoppable", and a Dream Life Designer.

As a coach, my mission is to help thousands of women build their identities and live their lives with love and respect.

Everything is possible because of "PURPOSE". In this way, I found my purpose to be the true essence of my life. I found the power to overcome any challenge coming my way.

## How does my purpose serve me?

As I decided to be the light for others, I could not go into darkness myself. Helping them makes me feel worthy, automatically. I am getting respect and love from my relatives, family, friends, and society. I have a reason to wake up every day, to become very productive and focused.

As I focus on a more significant cause, all great things are happening to me. The law of attraction works every single time. My vision is to transform the lives of millions of women and remain in their hearts forever. I will leave a legacy behind for generations that will make my family proud of me. I am living my dream, fulfilling, and incredible life. I will be committed to my purpose till my last breath.

One day every woman will live a meaningful, joyful life with purpose, and God will be proud of His creation.

**Sonali Kothari:**
https://linktr.ee/CoachSonali

An initiative of Mental Resilience Mastery © 2022

## PERFECT TIMING

Nurturing my inner strength has always been my power to become the best version of myself. My Purpose is to help people realize their inner strength, empower their self-talk, and become change-makers.

*"Don't settle for what life gives you; make life better and build something."*
*-Ashton Kutcher*

I always wanted to create my Identity. I was an average student and obedient child born in a joint family. Fun, happiness, traditions, and hearing NO were part of my life. I had big dreams but didn't have the courage or confidence to fulfil them. It's pretty exciting to look back over the homely Shy homemaker is now an independent woman, a special educator, and a transformational coach.

My mom always encouraged me to learn new things. Her routine started from the morning at 4 o'clock till night at 10 o'clock, but she still made time to teach my brother the values of life and me. Her habit of reading books and keeping herself updated with time inspired me to do the same.

When I sat and wrote this chapter, I was always on Purpose, which evolved as I matured.

With every visit to temples and respect to rituals, my only ask for God is, "why am I here? There should be some reason you have to send me on this earth; please show me the purpose of my birth".

When I got married, I wholeheartedly took the responsibility to build a loving home for my family and children. As making a difference is one of the intrinsic values, I carry in myself. I was keen on nurturing a family with values, love, and discipline in whatever way I could. I enjoyed the process of family life, but somewhere Being a pacemaker by nature, inner peace was essential for me, and there came a phase in my life where I was ultimately in chaos. Although everyone where they are around me, I felt incomplete within myself. I felt stuck. My brain was chattering about family expectations, parents, and friends. It was a point where I looked in the mirror and asked myself, "If I were to die one month from today, what would I do, and how would I want to be remembered? What legacy do I want to leave?"

These questions shook me, and I gathered myself, "To be the change that I wanted to see in the world."

When I moved a step forward, I had so many fingers pointing at me, telling me *A mother of two children has no time to pursue her dream.
* At the age of 38, it's too late to pursue a career
* How selfish you are trying to escape from your family responsibilities.
*You are born with a silver spoon, so why do you want to go back for money? *You are married, and your husband is your Identity.

The list goes on! Yes, these comments did affect me. I couldn't avoid criticism, but I chose to live with that and not allow it to affect me anymore.

An initiative of Mental Resilience Mastery © 2022

*"Maturity is when you stop complaining and making excuses and start making changes."*

All credit goes to my habit of reading books before sleeping inspired me to move forward against all the odds.

I enjoyed challenging myself every time, and this kept me going. One day, when I went to pick up my son from school, I saw a mother shouting horribly at a child. She was making him scared by lighting a matchstick. I was nervous that she may not harm the child in anger. After talking to his mother, I learned that he studies 24/7 but still scored only single-digit scores in exams. I discovered he had a learning disability, which made me curious about the child.

It was then I decided to help the child. I got certified in special education. The journey of working with these children made me more vital every day. There was also the time I felt exhausted and irritated for not giving the result as expected. But every smile I received and every blessing from my parents kept me going.

We are constantly growing and changing, and our experiences inspire us to shift directions; this is what exactly happened with me. I gradually connected with these children's parents and felt they needed attention and help. The self-talk these people had with themself was so discouraging that it damaged their lives. Where ever I am now is only because of what I say to myself in good and bad times. By empowering self-talk chattered in my mind, **"I can do it, just do it."**

As very well said, "the universe will show you the way; you just have to have the guts to go there."

I chose to explore the world of transformational coaching and discovered my core values. I started working on every area of my life. I took full responsibility for creating the result. I empowered my inner wisdom and became the full version of myself. People can withstand just about anything as long as they have a purpose to persevere.

In general, we spend most of our time adjusting and compromising, developing coping mechanisms to accept life, playing a blame game, giving excuses, procrastinating, and having low self-belief stop us from living our life to the fullest potential. Many times, we have a vision but no clear plans. No clarity about how to make things possible. I truly understand this, as I have also spent many valuable years with a limiting mindset. It's never too late, and I was lucky enough to work on my perspective, accelerating my personal growth and being the game-changer of my life. Nothing happens; by magic, and it cannot happen without taking the first move. Aligning your thoughts with your action signifies being in the best state. The key is to get started and gain momentum.

Now I am on a mission to help millions of people to enjoy their authentic selves and become the best version of themselves. Making people aware of their core self helps them believe in their inner strength. Create a balance to live a happy, harmonious life.

**Alka Oswal:**

**https://mez.ink/alka.oswal82**

**SMILE-THE COVETED ARMOUR**

An initiative of Mental Resilience Mastery © 2022

*"Listen with curiosity. Speak with honesty. Act with integrity. The greatest problem with communication is we don't listen to understand. We listen to reply (respond/react). When we listen with curiosity, we don't listen with the intent to reply. We listen for what's behind the words."*
— Roy T. Bennett, The Light in the Heart

It is the most playful time of the year, summer vacations. I love going to school; every hour, the subject change, now and then the chapter change, and even every year, the class teacher change. I like change, and I like holidays only when travel destinations change. Apart from the episode of my daily watch during the summer vacation, nothing seems to change! After completing all self-reliant homework lists in the first two days of the holidays, all I have is a group of friends to visit and play along with every day. Some surprise visits happen from other classmates and my favourite visitor (Pishi), yet I expect and anticipate so much that the actual visit becomes very predictive; blame my hyper-creative mind! As per my mom, most of my friends are either more soft-spoken, intelligent, hardworking, disciplined, driven, or fair-skinned than me! To me, I am more bored than all of them summed together.

Confusing? Oh, This is me, in my primary school days, and I am sharing one particular day, and for a crucial reason, I chose this day to share! So, let's begin in the fairy tale way my life as my dad's princess has been.

Once upon a time, on a hot summer afternoon, sitting at the window pane of our home's first floor was, I, the youngest daughter of the house, staring at the empty lane, empty playground, and the home of the friend across the street. Hearing the soft snores of my family taking their afternoon nap, consumed by thoughts from heaven to hell, impossible for even the Gods to fathom, my main focus was sighting the first sign of any friend who could accompany me in riding the bicycle. I started the affinity to ride last year at Christmas, and as it happens, it is a standard ride for the adults, and all I have yet done in the previous six months is to balance it with my hands and walk beside it and help paddle it through empty roads. So, frankly, I don't yet ride it per se, yet I am in my first standard for divinity's sake. Finally, the first sounds of my parents waking up came by and attracted my attention, and in a few mins more, the door locks will open, and I could drag my friends out!

10, 9, 8, 7...

Your gatekeepers are more potent than your thoughts. Not being in control of your words is more powerful than what life and others do to you. Have the ultimate control over your intention!

6, 5, 4, 3...

Friendship is a ship that never sinks, the only boat that never sinks howsoever fierce the storm be in life. Whether a 3 am friend, movie friend, shopping friend, introspection friend, or study buddy, each is important and plays a vital role in our wellbeing. A single person cannot play all the functions and can't be omnipresent; hence all of them have their importance. It's true; nothing can replace a genuine friendship, but when our chaddi-buddy cannot make it, the shopping friend uplifts our mood just by being there. Hence, 'Har Ek Friend Zaruri Hota Hai' (Each friend is significant).

An initiative of Mental Resilience Mastery © 2022

2, 1... Rush!!

As soon as mom opened the door, I rushed out of the house towards my friend's house across the road with my giant bicycle, balancing it and not looking at anything other than the house I wanted to reach. Somewhere in the middle of the road, I lost my senses, not knowing what had happened.

Three hours after this incident, I finally comprehended that I was met with a (minor) accident where two people had crashed into me with my cycle. Though they were unscathed, I was crushed between three cycles and got bruises, unable to speak due to a scream that damaged my larynx, and unable to form words because of the shock. As a six-year-old, I only enjoyed moving from one lap to another for the next three days while the adults around were going crazy. On the fourth day, I made my first ever communicative smile, as in a smile by which I was talking to others. I initiated using a smile to express my words, not only as a gesture. At the age of ten, knowing from my experience that smiles, tears, gestures, and eye-rolling can communicate much faster than the said words.

In the later few years of schooling, I learned the impact of body language in human communication through various languages and communication programs. I groomed myself yet always took this ability as a tool to grow and succeed (Getting grades, winning over friends and friends, being cute after mischief, etc.). Those were my formative years; hence using every skill as a tool was the way I knew. After I got a formal job and again experienced boredom, this time a different kind, I first thought of the purpose of life, the day's goal, the aim of each of my actions, and word-oriented. I had a lot of space in my idle mind in corporate work-life. I went deeper each day with these thoughts; the purpose of my life peeled itself like an onion, each peeling came with a set of discomfort, and only once I accepted the associated pain did a deeper meaning unfold.

Without my planning or intentions, this phase of life came where my purpose was to spread the smile's strength and impact each individual, I interact with in a way that smiles help them become stronger each day.

An initiative of Mental Resilience Mastery © 2022

Did my purpose change before? Yes, will it change later? Yes!!

That's the beauty of life, the purpose is the face of our intention and faces change, and intention is the energy! I intend to make the world a better place to stay and experience than yesterday. My purposes will take faces as well as when needed and collaborate with similar purposeful people. Together humanity will make the world a better place!

While you need to wait for my autobiography to read each phase of the evolving me and my purpose, I let my goal change its face each time a turn (defining; good or bad) happens in my life. The underlying impact remains the same with the minimalist God-given human attributes to be human always and encourage more of humanity in the world.

*My dad said:* **"Being a human, you inherit having all the features of a human, the heart of humanity, and the power of mind that can analyse and feel at a high level of coherence. You are my child. I am human, and the only thing you inherit is the human. The rest is up to you.**

These words became my permanent source of hope and light, guiding me through the darkest times.

I go by the name Dr Sumana/ Sumana, and I am reachable via: **https://linktr.ee/ask2dr.sumana.**

**Always happy to help!!**

An initiative of Mental Resilience Mastery © 2022

## MISSION POSSIBLE- SEARCH AND

## FOUND

*Donate a smile by helping individuals take charge of life, nurture relations & cultivate growth.*

I often think about the purpose behind the existence of stars, planets, sun, earth, and numerous non-living and living things. What is the purpose of human existence? I am sure there is a reason behind everything. I assume that a thing's presence leads to another's existence. And so, to find the reason for its existence is like finding the basis for everything.

Similarly, to find the purpose of human existence, we must find the purpose of all the things that have led to the presence of humans. Or, we can say that the purpose of living beings is to live. The goal of all beings is to exist. We are fit to be human if we know how to live.

A honey bee knows to gather nectar and make a honeycomb all her life.
A sparrow knows to collect straws of grass to make her nest.
A ball knows to bounce.

An initiative of Mental Resilience Mastery © 2022

A wheel knows to rotate.

## What does a human being know?

It amazes me that humans are the only species that give unique answers to this question. If you ask any ant on this planet, "what is your purpose?" the only answer we might get is to collect food and build an ant hill. But every human has a different purpose in living. Some might say they want to create tall buildings; for some, the goal is to write; for others might be to mend machines, treat other people, live happily, etc.

*My life's purpose is to help people realise their purpose and transform their lives.*

For a girl born, bought up & married in a typical Marwadi family, the "*purpose*" is imposed by default.
As a daughter, I had to follow family culture, agree with elders and keep them happy by conforming to their rules.
As a mother, I had to nurture kids.
As a student, I had to complete graduation just to get married.
As a wife and daughter-in-law, I had to look after the family and maintain social relationships.

**This question always hit me; is it an assigned role in a movie that I need to complete to make it robust and prove myself to be the best performer in all positions to get an Oscar award? How long should it go on, and for how long should I prove myself? Is it Nisha's purpose, or it's a role play?**

I was not given the right to choose or take any decision. Freedom of taking charge was not available. Asking for space to think was rebellious against the family values and culture. A girl with a dark complexion who never got the opportunity to go to English medium school, nor the freedom to choose a groom or express her feelings, had a passion and dream. A girl who has seen suffering, dominance and gone through hurts that could not be shared and trauma that cannot be expressed dared to know the dream and take action for what she deserved. Since childhood, I have felt the need for freedom, independence, and safe boundaries attached to values and culture.

With some doubts & resistance around, my journey started as a school teacher in a small town. The learning I gave students was much broader than the subject I taught students. Being a teacher allowed me to learn child psychology and interact with parents regularly. I developed a rapport with the parents to guide them on parenting to bring out the best in students. This made me popular among parents, and I soon realised that I was meant to be more than just a teacher. I started public speaking on the topics such as family relations, effective public speaking and parenting. It allowed me to enter NGOs, corporates and other more prominent educational institutes. I kept learning, upgrading, cross-skilling and upskilling myself by learning alternate therapies, NLP, counselling, etc. All this became possible due to the support I received from my family, friends and mentors. And somewhere along the journey, I discovered that transforming people's lives by helping them bring awareness, acceptance, and clarity brings the most joy to me. It adds more meaning to my life. That which makes me happy and brings sense to my life is my purpose.

I am Nisha Chandak, a brand of simplicity and courage.
I have seen skilful, talented students, women and men with a lot of potential but living in frustration, individual depression, emotional setback, feeling ignored, unloved and unaccepted. They all have dreams, know their calibre, and have all the resources but are still unable to take

courageous actions because of mind conditioning and limiting beliefs. They are evident and keep talking about what they don't want and don't like. The only thing they don't know is what they are looking for in life. What will make them happy What's? their ultimate purpose in life? They are trapped in their self-created cage, locked by fear of the unknown, which never allows them to take charge of life and step towards their purpose.

How do I achieve my purpose? It is through the medium of interactive sessions and life-transforming mentoring programs.

Through my mastermind, **"Shakhs se Shakhsiyat** – *A journey from person to personality"*, –I wish to empower individuals to take charge of life with clarity, courage and compassion by tapping into inner power. Every person can become a personality which will be remembered as long as there are humans on earth. I wish to shoot their mental blocks, destroy their limiting beliefs, and declutter their minds to open them up to their potential without boundaries.

My signature workshop – *"Aparajita – A power lady"*, revolves around empowering women not to compete with men but to respect and mark their existence.

An initiative of Mental Resilience Mastery © 2022

It is the process to discover self.
Define identity.
Design Legacy.
It is the process of living freely with responsibilities.
To remind us that a woman is the backbone of a family.
By empowering women, I wish to emancipate the backbone of society. This will lead to healthy relationships, happy families, content individuals, and peaceful society.

*"Design Your Death"* – My upcoming book & workshop prepares an individual to live life to the fullest.

Sounds ironic!

Designing death is the way to live a happy, fulfilling, well-planned and efficient life. We take life for granted so much that we tend to forget that we have a limited life span. The count down to death had already begun at the time of birth. We procrastinate in taking action on our dreams. We even procrastinate in expressing our feelings. The countdown doesn't stop.

The time keeps on ticking.
Death keeps on nearing.

An initiative of Mental Resilience Mastery © 2022

And when it knocks on the door, we are not ready.
Ask yourself this; are we living a life that will lead to a legendary death?
Will people remember us even after hundreds of years of our death?
Will I be fully content and satisfied at the time of my death?
All we do is live life by default.
Die by default.

I pursue to empower people to design their death so they can live a life of their choice.

People often forget that the essential thing in life is happiness and give more importance to other material or immaterial aspects. "Design Your Death" is how to program ourselves for a happy and lively Life. We plan for many life milestones; however, we never plan about the most certain thing in life; death. Life must lead to a guilt-free, peaceful, happy and fantastic end. Financial, relationship, social and spiritual goals need to be planned with the exact alignment. The workshop cum mentoring program very ably helps with this. It completely changes the perspective of the participants toward life positively. "Design Your Death" teaches about life in a true sense.

An initiative of Mental Resilience Mastery © 2022

There is no greater joy for me except seeing people's lives get better; they become happier and grow their lives. The abovementioned mediums will help me reach those people and impact their lives. Every purpose is incomplete without action. And action needs an execution plan. I plan to create a tribe of leaders that can carry out my purpose. That's how I wish to design my death by creating a legacy. My purpose shall remain and impact people even aeons after I am gone. Because purpose in itself is an inanimate idea. What gives purpose meaning are the people who carry it. The passion with which they take it spreads it and achieves it. And it will benefit the giver as well as the receiver.

**What a gift to have!**

**Nisha Chandak:**
https://linktr.ee/nishachandak

## PURPOSE OF LIFE IS A LIFE OF

## PURPOSE

As I perceive it, life is not simply to come into human birth and live blindly as this world's Maya/ Illusion dictates and die one day without contributing to making the world any better. Neither is it to be lived simply as per experiences one gathers and behave measure-to-measure as per how others behaved with you (especially not those negative experiences!). Nor can it be about grabbing all you can in greed or being on a power-wielding trip - living like a mindless zombie causing widespread destruction, leaving the world uglier than one found! What then is life's purpose?

Reflecting on my growing-up days, though I pranced around as a happy-go-lucky curious kid, there was a lot of the ugly, painful, and unhealthy that occupied my personal space as a constant destructive force. One carries a lot from childhood experiences that later become life-defining. I have borne the consequences of the wreckage caused by the presence of a narcissistic and abusive father and queer silence of a docile mother. Both parents were working, and even though the existential requirements: living, tuition, food, and clothing were well-managed, the underlying dysfunction was easy to note. The mental-emotional picture being created constantly in my subconscious memory was downright dreary! Negative experiences I underwent were hardly ever counter-balanced with happy memories. To date, I don't remember communicating ever on a positive note with my father, and I never understood why! Break-point came, and all hell broke loose as I touched my teenage years. The aftermath of being in the eye of a storm still shows up as tight spots requiring self-loving, empathetic navigation each time! It's been a tumultuous journey:

- Learning to keep my sanity.
- Learning to shift focus away from annihilating.
- Destructive energies.
- Learning not to get caught up in other people's drama.

The intense suffering at a young age took me to hell and back before transforming itself into becoming a source of strength: helping me reclaim my soul from the dark side, moving me beyond operating in the victim mode, away from very close calls with living a life marred with destructive, unhealthy addictions.

An initiative of Mental Resilience Mastery © 2022

In 2004, I came across this book titled *"Man's Search for Ultimate Meaning",* where the author Viktor Emil Frankl summed up his life lessons. He hailed the search for life's meaning as a "central human motivational force". He wrote this book to further his reflection process on his varied life experiences, including surviving the Holocaust. The topics of spirituality and layers of self he touched upon were of deep interest. From him came the inspiration to take the path of "self-reflection" to find my true North. Though many of his concepts were beyond my understanding back then, his book still profoundly impacted me, making me wish I had read it earlier.

According to Viktor Frankl, discovering one's life purpose has a pre-requisite existential analysis, which needs to be coupled with RESPONSIBILITY. The inner-self constantly comes into clarity and awareness through self-reflection. The onus of taking that deep dive to grow inwards and reach their life purpose falls uniquely on each individual. As per Frankl, that is how the soul takes on a constant inner journey of moving from an "unconscious instinctual self" to the "conscious spiritual self"!

Though my search for meaning in human existence and deeper truths had begun early, I candidly admit lacking any sense of responsibility. Constant bouts of frustration and rebellion ensued without any healthy outlets. Many mind blockages manifested due to a lack of self-reflection or mindful responsiveness to triggers, but I didn't know any better! Being a Holocaust survivor, Frankl noted the blatant truth about suffering being a double-edged sword. Suffering can cease to feel like suffering when some "meaning" is attached to it, which can lead to positive outcomes. He then goes on to warn against getting stuck in a fatalistic quagmire! "Unnecessarily Suffering is masochistic rather than heroic!" he said. I later learned how deeply cathartic kicking unnecessary suffering could be: drawing lines, ending certain toxic relationships while making new ones, thus creating consciously one's support system and the space for one's self-worth to shine through. It became part of my life purpose: keeping human dignity at the forefront of everything. Not suffering yourself, neither carry that energy forward, thus breaking that chain - that toxic behavioural pattern. Learning to create boundaries with others has no doubt been highly self-empowering. Regaining soul-strength starts to transpire when one says NO to all that is disempowering!

My professional journey was never linear: I hopped from a marketing job in a car company to public relations stint at the Italian Embassy, to working with NGOs, to consulting for foreign companies creating a base in India, and completing my Exec MBA from France in 2016 and working as Strategy Consultant with budding entrepreneurs. I have been on a roller-coaster unregretfully on learning curves and have constantly added to my soul lessons. Now amalgamating all that experience towards becoming a Business and Power Mindset Coach, life has come to the point of convergence. The choice of training myself to become a Mindset Coach reinforced itself as a self-transformational decision too. Those blind spots** which went unseen earlier, leaving me depleted and defeated, no longer affect me much as I bounce back faster. (**A special note of thanks to Coach David Nair for crucial insights and breakthroughs that helped me take bountiful leaps of faith!) I now understand, with clarity, my RESPONSIBILITY towards keeping my balance even though nothing or nobody else will be by my side (nobody except God!).

My inner journey has thus evolved. I have become deeply self-aware, soul-connected, and heart-connected. One step at a time, moving from an "unconscious instinctual self" into my "conscious spiritual self"! In tandem with this profound journey inwards, I feel slowly yet powerfully inching towards "self-actualization" - the highest purpose as a soul journeying this human matrix. Unwavering faith in the Supreme Kavir Saheb has helped mould my life learnings to an enormous extent by unveiling subtle karmic truths. He continues to impact my life each moment with His constant presence. His peaceful grace is the only place my soul has learned to be in total surrender.

A humble, spiritual way of life has thus become my existential TRUTH. Though the same truth applies to humanity at large, only whence a soul is fully awakened, and enlightened does the ability to acknowledge this truth manifest. The current downturn of value systems that human beings face today with widespread destruction, death, and disease, is an ugly pointer that we all refuse to acknowledge: lack of faith in the Supreme! Unless humans spiritually awaken and confidence in the ONE Supreme is restored, the future will get even more contorted than today! This one thought is enough to prod me into action and binds me deeply with my purpose in life. Karmic and spiritual insights have added to a strong WHY in my life, nudging me to honour my learnings, creating an impactful life purpose and giving back to humanity.

Today, I believe I'm wiser. More adept at going through the process of self-reflection and consciously delving within to search for answers. I have learned that three things must align to create one's life purpose: core values, inner strengths, and innate passions, and learning how to catapult them to be of service to humanity, thus finding one's "Ikigai"! ('Iki' in Japanese means' life,' and 'gai' describes value or worth.) While training to become a coach, I also discovered my core values: Intuition, Truth, Empathy, and Refinement. My strengths are my clarity of thought and ability to provide insights to help people deep-dive, reflect and transform their lives. I am super passionate about the process of metamorphosis, of deep inner transformations. My findings continue to gear me in defining my purposeful life. "Person of Influence" to help empower every human soul that I can touch, to help individuals dive deeper into their spiritual self, creating self-empowerment and self-realisation as their reality. Moreover, generate impact through my life story of overcoming hardship and transformation, inspiring youth and women to "Mphosize" ("metamorphose") themselves through masterminds, books, talks, etc. Furthering the most crucial lesson of life: Silence disempowers, communication empowers.

I thus intend to live my "LIFE OF PURPOSE" to the fullest by being of service to humanity - be it a cause, individuals, or community. Furthermore, remain in surrender to that ONE Supreme, acquire Eternal abundance of the soul, and leave the world a little more refined and beautiful than I found it. The quest of finding my life purpose has gone beyond simply being a professional success story! It is instead about becoming an empowered, enlightened human being - mind, body, and soul and creating a legacy that continues beyond this lifetime.

This journey called "LIFE" is short and will be over sooner than one can fully comprehend it. Leaving no reasons to spend another second living a life that isn't meaningful, authentic, and does not serve society and humanity at large! If your soul resonates with painting your Eternal canvas while living a life of soulful significance and leaving behind a legacy for future generations.

Reach out
**Shikha Singh**
**at** https://linktr.ee/coachshikha for a collaborative, mutually empowering connection.

## MY CRAZY DREAMS

### Bio Dr Rajiv Agarwal

I am Dr Rajiv Agarwal, founder of "You and Wealth" mastermind. I am a loving husband of an accomplished software professional, wife, and family—an employee, CFO, consultant, startup investor, etc. My vision is to help people improve their relationship with money & create a blueprint for their financial independence. I am PhD in Finance and am the author of a book on money, finance, and wealth.

My professional journey has seen many highs and lows. I have bounced back from adversity with greater strength. I became financially independent at 45 years. My passion is supporting educational needs, and I have helped over 350 students in the last 18 years. I invested in a startup by providing seed capital and scholarships to needy students—I served United Nations for 18 years in Iraq, South Sudan, Somalia, and Kenya.

Dr Rajiv Agarwal PhD. Finance, Cost accountant, Company Secretary, SAP-certified consultant 1. Finance and Admin

head with UNFAO 18 years in Iraq, South Sudan, Somalia 2. CFO in the Corporate sector for ten years in India
3. Finance expert
4. Business and Wealth coach
5. SAP ERP consultant
6. Research project for the edible oil industry in Kenya
7. Owner of Beautiful money Mastermind

**Purpose of my life**

My first purpose is to develop ten financial strategies for different financial assets to build wealth. Test these ten strategies on live financial markets with my own money. Refine them and standardize them with my experience. Create ten systems for ten designs describing the mindset and skill set required to achieve the desired results. Describe the profile of the person for whom each system can be adopted and the steps he needs to complete before implementing that system. This inspiration I took from the book Complete Turtle Trader by Michael W. Covel. In this book, All fresh graduates were selected to trade other people's money and were getting a commission to implement the strategy given to them. None of them had the capital to start trading, nor did they have any experience in trading. In 5 years, everyone was a multi-milliner, building wealth for themselves with their own money. Conditions have changed a lot. Stock markets have matured. Big institutions from India and other countries are involved in a big way. Domestic and foreign institutions are trading in India to build wealth for their investors. I will develop strategies for people of different mindsets. The objective of implementing procedures will be to achieve financial independence early in life.

## Why first purpose

I have spent 35 years getting knowledge and experience in finance and investment. I have acquired a skill set in developing financial and investment strategies for different assets and done my research project to maximize the return for one industry for a country as a whole. I know the process. How can the strategy be developed and tested? How can the industry implement them? I am also an investor and trader in the Indian share market and study financial analysis of world markets and how they impact Indian markets. I love reading books. My area of interest in reading is financial strategies and success in life.

After acquiring and applying this knowledge for myself, becoming financially independent, and smoothly travelling on the path to building wealth, however, I was implementing that path for myself. Two years before, I thought now I was ready to pay back to society. However, I do not have a system to deliver my knowledge. I Want to help the community. I started exploring how I could start this journey. I am always ready to learn new skills in life. To achieve the outcome of my vision, I joined Mr Arfeen Khan, a world-renown coach program on speak to fortune and "Book to fortune." I have written a book, Path of building wealth, and started the journey to impact the lives of people in the age group of 20 to 55 years in India and abroad.

## The outcome of the first purpose

The outcome of the first purpose will be to move 10000 people from middle class to upper-middle class every year to become financially independent, achieve their dreams, and give new plans to the next generation. The mission can be accomplished by spreading financial awareness through workshops, TV shows, and FM Radio and delivering keynote speeches on strategies and systems to build wealth. There will also have an impact on the GDP of the country.

## My 2nd purpose in life

An initiative of Mental Resilience Mastery © 2022

My 2nd purpose is to develop one strategy to achieve excellence in any one of the sports selected in time for children. Develop a system with this strategy so that one who wants to cultivate the idea of becoming an international level player what parents should do and when.

**My Why for 2nd purpose**
I was inspired to become a cricket player. I dedicated my first ten years to playing and improving without knowledge of what is required to become a player and also struggling with finances for playing. I was carrying this dream in me and thought that money would not be a problem for my son and daughter and would inspire them to play. Same without the system, I was aware but not clear that starting time for any kid to achieve excellence in sports is 3 to 4 years. Activities and environments must be given from age 1 to accomplish the objective. My son was an outstanding player in tennis, and my daughter was good at gymnastics. However, the focus was divided between study and sports, and skill development started at 10-11, which was still late. Now I am developing a system that I will refine and test with my granddaughter to inspire her to become a great international player in any game.

The system will guide for the next 15 years.

## The outcome of the 2nd purpose

Inspiration for me to develop this system is to improve India's Olympic tally of medals in Gold, Silver, and Browns by 300% from the last Olympics in the next 15 years. My inspiration is when USA and China can do why not India? The system will provide sufficient information for parents. Parents will understand the steps required at different ages children. We need to build awareness on a micro level and implement it through public awareness. I am working on this project and preparing my granddaughter and other children for our next generation.

An initiative of Mental Resilience Mastery © 2022

**Dr Rajiv Agrawal:**
**https://linktr.ee/agarwal.rajiv22**

## MY HAPPINESS QUOTIENT

I am Supriya Rane, a law graduate and entrepreneur. I am currently working in the hospitality industry in India. I had the privilege of working in the corporate banking world in Australia for ten years. Both roles are service-oriented and exposed me to work and interact with people from diverse backgrounds and different cultures. I am also a coach, speaker and the author of *Keen Agers - No Age Limit on Life.* This book was written and published in Covid times, as I was deeply touched by the plight of older adults during the Covid-19 pandemic.

We all are looking for our purpose in life. Once connected to the drive, a sense of direction and meaning to life is achieved. My passion is to bring a smile and spread happiness in the lives of people I touch. As

I explored my purpose, I found more reasons to work in this untapped area of life, especially in India -that of seniors. As lifespans are increasing, planning life in the third quarter of life is gaining importance.

The Covid-19 pandemic and complete lockdown posed unprecedented challenges for healthy living for all age groups but more so among seniors globally. It highlighted gaps, especially for the elderly who live alone. I saw my parents struggle with no maids and sometimes deal with limited food supplies and medicines. I was not allowed to visit them as there were movement restrictions, and they were in isolation because of their vulnerability to external infection. Most seniors live in nuclear families and face loneliness as children have left the nest for better prospects overseas. Some did not even have a partner due to the death of a spouse or divorce. I feel it is time to shift our focus on people, not material things, to do something new, progressive and empowering.

I found my purpose: to help seniors realise the importance of healthy ageing, where they are continually reinventing themselves as they pass through the landmark years of sixty to eighty years and beyond. It means finding new things to enjoy, learning to adapt and being socially and physically active.

My mission is to create awareness so that society is educated and engaged in helping seniors live happy and healthy life and create a favourable environment.

Today freedom and independence of doing what you want and how you wish to live your retired life have become the most significant differentiators for seniors.

Healthy relationships need compromise, respect, trust and support. Both seniors and their children need "to being supported and the supporter."

Here are some pointers I am focusing on where the community can pitch in. Education and awareness are the keys to achieving this.

1. There is always a starting point from where we currently are, and it is never too late to live the life one always dreamt of. It is time to free oneself from the chains of worry and not be a pendulum in others' hands. Do not let others' expectations cage you, and do not worry about being judged.

By being socially active and pursuing creative ways to occupy, seniors can overcome loneliness and improve bonding with people who are on the same page and same destination. Associating with the right people gives insights and options for dealing with challenges and opens your mind to new possibilities so that you are not alone in life's journey.

2. Communities can participate through sponsorship; professionals can volunteer and give free health, fitness, yoga and meditation lectures. Also, arranging counselling sessions to help seniors deal with grief is essential. Fun group activities such as picnics, visits to cultural programs, dramas, museums, exhibitions, and theatres, help to socialize and bond with one another.

3. If re-employment after retirement is managed with the support of government bodies, churches and the local community welfare schemes, seniors can add to their income, earning respect. This creates a sense of physical, mental and emotional well-being. Part-time admin roles, managing accounts, giving tuitions, gardening, and growing organic fruits and vegetables are some ways to generate revenue.

I have a classic example where an older woman made excellent homemade sweets and gave them away as gratitude to the youth helping her buy food and medical supplies during the Covid-19 lockdown. Soon her sweets became the talk of the neighbourhood, and she obtained orders for snacks and sweets. Her business was a success as shops, sweet marts were closed, and there was a high demand for home-cooked food.

4. Regular health checkups, exercise, yoga and diet awareness are crucial and can be arranged by Rotary clubs, where doctors volunteer to be a part of the medical camps as part of their contribution to society.

5. The concept of senior living homes, nursing homes, and home care are fast growing in India. It becomes a challenge when children settle abroad, with little help around. However, the demand is far higher than the supply. Innovative schemes and government involvement in assigning projects with subsidies for nursing homes are necessary. Businesses and property developers can also construct some luxury nursing homes for the affluent.

6. Financial literacy for women is paramount. Another characteristic of working Indian women is relying on their fathers or husbands to make financial decisions. Owning responsibility and controlling your money is one of the significant steps to feeling empowered. Most women are unaware of the family's investments, financial liabilities, insurance and other financial decisions.

It is unfortunate that after the sudden death of the husband, the wife has hardly any idea about where and how her husband invested when he was alive. To avoid such situations, women should insist on being part of the financial planning process for the family right from the start. The first step in financial independence is to personally visit banks for deposits, withdrawals and other transactions. Learn internet banking to carry out bank operations from home. Use an ATM card and credit card freely; this will boost your confidence. Meet your family tax advisor, financial planner and legal advisor in person to keep you updated with the latest position.

Embracing old age and preparing for it is essential. Life is a paradox. Everyone wants to live a long life, but growing old does not appeal to anyone. This is attributed to age-old stereotype thinking, where one feels like a victim, a burden on the family and society.

How about learning to live abundantly with less and exploring the possibilities of making old age a simple, fun and joyful experience?

For that, one needs to reframe the mind and focus on:

What is the one thing I will do today to begin the life I love?

Or

How do I leave a legacy?

Or

What is excellent in my life now that I have forgotten?

Or

How can I find the resources to keep myself creatively occupied and busy? "Do not regret growing old, it is a privilege denied to many" -*Unknown*

Ageing is a blessing and should be celebrated. There is a lot of grace, wisdom and maturity as one age. The focus shifts from perfection to pursuing your passion, and the journey is more important than the destination.

The highest sense of self-worth comes with experience and sensible choices. It is time to reward and pamper oneself for working and retirement savings. It is time to make yourself the number one priority, open your bucket list, and start doing what was once at the back of your mind.

My motto in life: "Love and respect seniors as you are aging too".

My mission is to create awareness so that society is educated, and engaged in helping seniors live happy and healthy life. It is a significant task, and a shift in focus is required to help add value and significance and transform the way society views ageing.

Would you like to be a part of this new offering and contribute, support, and help create a better world for seniors???

An initiative of Mental Resilience Mastery © 2022

**Supriya Rane:**
**https://linktr.ee/supriyarane**

## NOURISHING A DELICIOUS LIFE

I was born in Zimbabwe sixty years ago; I was a "laat lammetjie", loosely translated as a "late little lamb", several years after my siblings; being the only girl, I was naturally spoiled rotten. But what I wanted was the attention of my older brothers. And I would do anything to get it. I remember them telling me to bring them coffee in bed – so early in the morning, before anyone was up and about, I got up and went to the kitchen; now we lived on a farm and had a gas stove which required adult supervision to light. So boiling water was a slight dilemma. I had to resort to hot tap water with cold milk.

Not the best coffee!

Such was my determination. My Mother and I used to bake for the boys on a Thursday so they would have cookies and cakes for the weekend home from boarding school and fill "tuck" boxes on their return. Cooking was a way to give, show we cared, and celebrate family. It was a way of building a connection with others. And for me, a way of getting the much-desired attention from my brothers.

This fostered my love for food and hospitality. I love to serve people with warmth and generosity and give them the gift of pleasure, delicious food that looks appealing, and attentive service that makes them feel cared for, nurtured, and unique. When I opened my catering business, it was an opportunity to fulfil my love of food and hospitality and to help people create their dreams – beautiful, joyous weddings, successful corporate launches, fun-filled sporting events, and celebrations of any nature. It was gratifying to work long hours; with sore feet and backs, we worked when everyone else played. I had a young team of students who worked at events as waiters, waitresses and bartenders. These young people were always ready for fun and up to all kinds of mischief, so life was whole, and we thrived. The youngsters also aspired to be "more", and I loved helping them traverse their path to success – running their businesses and attaining industry firsts. Through the thirty years of running a catering business, we certainly had our times of feast and famine. There are so many memories, but that is another book. I do, however; doubtless, I delivered happiness, delight, satisfaction and many plates of food.

Navigating the entrepreneurial business for thirty years, I certainly experienced the trials and tribulations of being in business. Before opening my catering business, I had the opportunity to work as a troubleshooter in a very big industrial catering company, and it was gratifying:

- detecting problems and solving them came naturally; it is straightforward to pinpoint obstacles when you are not emotionally attached to the outcome, perhaps not when you are immersed in the issue yourself. There is an immense sense of accomplishment when we expose an obstruction and determine a solution. When you add creating a key to liberating and bringing a dream into fruition, then you know why you came to be there.

My mantra was, "Do it with love". Placed prominently in the business was the sign "Love". When I interviewed anyone, I was looking for people who loved food, loved doing things with passion and loved people. My philosophy is when you do it with love, you do it creatively filled with innovation; you enjoy it, it is satisfying and rewarding, it looks tempting and attractive, tastes delectable and feeds the soul – yours and theirs. So, on a deep level, my purpose is about nourishing the soul.

Working with people, such as employees, clients and suppliers, is fertile ground for learning. Over the years, I have learned much about human nature – mine and others. This is particularly prominent in the business ecosystem – it pulls into play the complexity of all our human needs, belief systems and inner programming. The realization of our dreams or watching the dreams fade and become a distant memory. How battles are fought and lost, or victories celebrated. Indeed, I have never been able to call life dull! But life itself has been a rich teacher. The many lessons I have learned in marriage, divorce, illness, grief and loss have armed me with compassion, empathy and wisdom.

After selling my catering business, I founded my coaching practice. I had studied to be a Success coach some years back, so I added another modality and embarked on another journey to understanding human nature – my own. It is like an onion; as you peel back one layer, another is revealed, one after the next. Just when you think you have a handle on it, another layer is exposed.

This journey of full disclosure is fundamental to my purpose. Understanding and accepting myself allows me to celebrate the diversity of others without judgment.

I see people accepting life – accepting mediocre and average as "that is just how life is". The door to possibility is firmly closed, and life is not lived fully. They accept circumstances like excess weight, job dissatisfaction, and mundane relationships as their "lot in life." Most people don't lead their life; they get it. They are not in love with life – they think showing up is enough. Being stuck in the illusion of limitation and victimhood is the set point for so many people.

Life doesn't have to be that way, and I see my purpose as opening the door to possibilities, poking "the bear" until he runs at life with passion and joy. To nourish their soul, they feel fully alive and live a life full of purpose, passion, vitality, curiosity and delight. To help people liberate their dreams and enable the belief that it is possible to achieve them. To help them clarify and identify their obstacles and develop a strategy to remove or circumvent them and illuminate and formulate their unique path to success.

After that, join them in celebrating not only their victories but also their delicious life. Changing one person's world can be the change that creates legacies for millions.

Jenni Jackson is a catalyst for change, a transformational success coach, an author, and a healer. She lives in Durban, South Africa, with her cat Chai.

Jenni qualified and trained as a teacher; food is her first love, so after qualifying, she worked as an operations manager for several catering companies until she started her own company. After thirty years in the catering business, she sold her business, intending to help people create lives rich with reward and accomplishment. Jenni is a passionate food-lover, social artist, avid reader, and soul feeder.

**Jenny Jackson:**
https://linktr.ee/coachjennijackson

An initiative of Mental Resilience Mastery © 2022

## THE MAGICAL TWINKLE

### The Defining Moment

That day was different. The moment was defining.

I woke up with the hustle and bustle noise, the rattling sound of crockery in the kitchen amidst laughter and voices of gratitude.

Hey, what was that, I wondered. So, I moved to the drawing room. And to my surprise found three visitors offering gratitude to my mother. This was, again, different. I thought my parents had reversed their roles.

What has my mom done for them? Why are they so grateful to her? Why are my mom's eyes glittering with joy? Probably the best twinkle I have ever seen in her eye. My father, by profession, is a hydropower expert pioneer in projects in India and neighbouring countries. This involved high-risk jobs for him and his team members. My mom complimented me by offering volunteer service to the victims of accidents. She would visit the victim's houses; work with the government officials for financial and emotional support. People would often come to express their gratitude, which was one such incident.

But this incident was quite different because the twinkle in her eye served as a trigger for a more meaningful living and magic thereof. And along the journey, I came out with the following;
My purpose in life is to live meaningfully and to be of significance.

During my life, I understood that we live only once. And so, my mom said, "Live so as you live only once". She felt that prayers are important and so is service and was deeply into voluntary service, prayers, etc. This served as a trigger for my purpose too.

My journey was full of challenges on the personal and professional front, and I lost many family members and decided to shift my pain to purpose. So, I continued with my plans to serve the community with my experiences and skills to lead the life I desire!!

My family supports my ventures, and I want to leave a legacy of "care and share."

**The Trigger:**
When I was a child, I read the book "Living with purpose" by Dr Radhakrishnan –the

former President of India, who stands tall like a colossus among the luminaries on the Indian horizon.

A noted philosopher, champion for freedom and educationist, his thoughts triggered me into the habit of thinking. I thought deeply into the purpose of living, the value of life, the existence of a higher force, and the ultimate destination of the flight. I decided to take charge of my life. I put down my questions in black and white. Having written me why a better clarity on vital issues started emerging. I probed life's journey in small baby steps, one step at a time. I located my passions through a meditative process. I aligned my forces with my mission. I chose HR as a profession due to its close affinity with my above parameters. I coined some affirmations to catapult me into action and keep me on track. Here are some
I'm living with a purpose.
My purpose is exciting.
My purpose gives me direction and consistency.

### Purpose and its effects

Ever since I was drawn into the realisation of living a meaningful life, my perspective towards events in life changed. I was able to evaluate situations more clearly and organise and reframe experiences. I responded to problems in a better and more mature way. This change was felt in the entire wheel of life.

I dealt with situations more proactively; I focused more on what I could do and appreciated what I had. I realised the other side of the grass is always greener.

The best part was that I stopped playing the victim card and took complete ownership of the decisions. I realised that I was the pilot of my life, and I could not allow anyone else to take charge of my life, and whenever I moved out of the tangent, my purpose pulled me back.

True fulfilment comes from designing your own life. This is how one unlocks the Extraordinary.

## The Journey

The journey along the road was bumpy and full of challenges, but somehow, I always believed that "A Rainbow is more powerful than the storm".

Here are some of the fierce challenges which I faced at the same time—

1) My son was the country's most premature child; he was called the miracle baby of PGI Chandigarh. Since his milestones were delayed, he required a

different kind of bringing up; this was a big challenge. Today he has completed his Hotel Management and is working for ITC Hotel.

2) My Father-In-law, an army officer, was on oxygen for four years. Being in the army, he was posted at very high altitudes, which affected his lungs.

3) My mother was detected with stage 4 cancer.

4) I was in a Media Job at the helm of affairs and was required 24*7.
I not only walked through these challenges but served as a role model for others.
I did not give up on my Dream Assignment, instead excelled despite all odds. On the flip side, I did not have time to overthink; I became a crisis manager at home and in the office. I became famous as a Go-to-person for solutions and managing emotions. I learnt to **dance in the rain,** which emerged as my **Unique Personality Skill.**

**OUTCOME: THERE ARE NO FAILURES, ONLY DETOURS.**
**The outcome of handling this crisis at one go changed my entire perspective and gave me the confidence to tread on rough patches. My belief turned into a**

**conviction "That there is a sunrise after every spell of darkness".**

**I started helping people with solutions, showcasing their options and encouraging them to follow their aspirations.**
**And I would often tell them—Kites fly against the winds, and success is a failure turned upside down**.

And when I saw the relief on their faces, I would be reminded of the brightest twinkle in my mom's eye.
So, I thought, why not share my experience and skills for creating a difference in people's lives by empowering them this further brought clarity to my "WHY".
This thought process has made my new outlook so robust that I have lost many battles but never a war. I can proudly say that I have achieved the toughest of milestones which were often considered impossible in each organisation I have worked for.

**New Why Evolved:**
I realised that purpose is a journey and not a destination.

'**We are all winners. It's just that, the journey is not easy**.'
An initiative of Mental Resilience Mastery © 2022

World over, people have one thing in common: they battle for their dreams.

We all fight with our circumstances, with our inner voices each day. Yes, we have the power for extraordinary, but we are shaken by the slightest of the winds of life. Most of us do not understand that this is a temporary phase in life and shall pass.

Perseverance is the key. I failed initially in some of my projects but learned the lessons, refocused, realigned the strategy, and rebounded with double the energy.

So, I would like to empower people to design the life they desire by moving out of the challenges and urging them not to abandon their dreams.

I want to leverage my experience, my skills to empower people to convert their setbacks to step-ups and reach New Heights. This would give meaning and significance to my life.

**My Purpose:**
**I want to work with people keen to move out of the setbacks and challenges and reorganise their toolkits to lead inspiring life.**
**It is not easy, but it is better to fight than to die with the music still in my heart.**
**My Vision:**
An initiative of Mental Resilience Mastery © 2022

I am on a mission to help thousands of people challenge their adversities and revive their dreams. I chip in as a catalyst to ignite the extraordinary lamp to create shifts and Reach New Heights.

In pursuit of the above, I have written a book by the Name of **"Warrior Revived"** This book is an inspiration to pursue one's dreams, despite setbacks.
It offers a combination of unique techniques to reframe identity with the help of the latest, well-researched toolkit to tighten up the loose ends to cross the barriers, face challenges, and fight to the finish.

I have been visiting various educational institutes and conducting webinars by showcasing to them the solutions I offer for stepping up their life.
To add more value, I run my Mastermind Programme **, New Heights,** with a group of people to empower them to develop strength and fortitude to overcome adversity, treat failures and rejections as events, make a new beginning with clear goals and cover that extra ground to be extraordinary.

**Dream again and live the life you are meant to!!**
An initiative of Mental Resilience Mastery © 2022

**Hence--**

"It is okay to Fail but it is not okay to Stay there,
It is okay to rest in Valleys, but it is not okay to not to scale the peaks,
It is okay to be Cautious, but it is not okay to live in fear,
It is okay to be Embarrassed, but it is not okay to live in guilt,
It is okay to be Rejected, but it is not okay to give up,
For you are Extraordinary, meant to play the music you so love... (Monica)..."

**Monica Sodhi:**
**https://linktr.ee/houseofreengineering**

# INFLUENCERS RECOMONDATION

"Thirty successful mentors, coaches, trainers and guides from Mental Resilience Mastery Mastermind have come together to publish the book "GRAIL- tick your life right, with Purpose". Each has contributed a chapter to showcase the Definite Major Purpose.

Many lack Purpose in their life, and as briefly detailed in Jane Goodall's book, "The greatest danger to our future is APATHY. "Others, such as Mahatma Gandhi and Mother Teresa who had their Purpose clearly defined, as we see in the work they left behind.

In my 60-year work experience, I feel "PURPOSE" is built on four pillars Ignorance, fear, weak early foundation and inability to change.

When one manages these four pitfalls, they can manage their mind, heart and soul in their search for PURPOSE.

An initiative of Mental Resilience Mastery © 2022

This book provides the Strength, Passion and Clarity (SPC formula ), which can help the community develop and sustain their PURPOSE. In so doing, make this World a better place for all of us. Hence I wholeheartedly recommend this book."

-Walter Vieira

*Walter Vieira pioneered marketing consulting in India and has been visiting professor In business schools in USA, Europe and SE Asia; author of 16 books on management; business columnist with Business World, Times, Express etc.; first President of Institute of Management Consultants of India; and first Asian elected Chairman of ICMCI, the world apex body of Management consultants.*

"It's unputdownable as you try to pause and reflect after reading every event. I lived through the stories as I moved from one word to another, with each tale touching the core of my soul. So, if you think there's an unconquerable mountain, this book is your trekking pole."

- Suresh Mansharmani

Founder, Tajurba Internationale
3 times TEDx Speaker

An initiative of Mental Resilience Mastery © 2022

# PASSION

## LOVE AND PASSION

I could not find out why people suffer emotionally, physically, and financially in our world. These feelings came to me from my childhood. A memory that stands out is: when there was a discussion between my mom and Gurudev, her Guru/Master, they were discussing poor and rich. I was in my 5th standard; I happened to say, "no one is poor, no one is rich, everything you get is from this earth, whether it is gold or diamonds or anything, it belongs to all of us; why is there a differentiation in all these things. Why do we condemn anybody with poverty? Why?" I felt this in my heart, and I expressed myself. I was bold, and they looked at me and said, "How do you see this? Do you understand what you are saying?" I said," Yes, we are all rich because the planet has given us everything we need, only we have not taken it properly. If I want to breathe, I breathe, there is no rationing to it, and if I want to eat, there is food provided; if I want to drink water, there is a provision. There is a place for me to rest; there is the earth." All these things made life very clear to me, but I saw people suffering endless suffering. I could not relate to why they suffered so much.

When you encounter a harrowing situation in life, you know you are vulnerable; you desperately look for a solution; that's what happened to me. My sister, who is 11 years younger than me, is my heart. And now she's diagnosed with blood cancer. She is a year-old mother who looks up to me and says, "Didi, I want to live." Faced with this situation and the challenge of finding a solution, I knocked on all the doors for help. I came across a Feng Shui master who gave me immense knowledge to unlock the energy of suffering. As a qualified Naturopathy Doctor, I could deep dive into acquiring knowledge as a Qi Gong practitioner Chiropractic Akashi, etc. Name it; I did everything I could find; This opened the Pathway to achieving life, and she survived. Today her son is an engineer, and she is living beautifully with God's grace.

In this journey of 26 years, I encountered many challenges but never gave up my belief, intense with faith and grace of God. I overcame all my challenges. One of my biggest challenges was my sister's health. When I saw her in so much pain, I brought her to my house. I looked after her every moment: her vomiting blood, unbearable pain, and child crying. What agony to go through, but I became stronger to face all this. I did not allow my emotions to be hijacked. At times, I locked myself in a room alone and emptied my heart. But never in front of anybody, I strengthened myself by facing each challenge as it appeared and faced my Warfield head-on; I became stronger and stronger. My path opened. Allopathic medicine was the first line of medicine; other elements only made the impact more effective for optimum healing. The power of positive energies diminishes the negative one. Of course, restoring my sister's health to normally took about 2 to 3 years. My passion for helping and finding a solution became my purpose in life.

I met a very Pious and knowledgeable Master. I went to Kailash; I met someone who came and spoke to me to take charge to overcome all agony of life as if I was appointed No Look Back; MY transformation of everyone was like the blooming of the flower. Today I see myself as a gardener to help everyone to prove their lives. That is what is happening. My purpose was to nurture love and happiness in everyone's life; this became very simple to reach out to others. Be an infant. Everything happens right now; My focus is to fulfil my journey. Only his deeds, whatever I have to do in my life and I have received from this planet, everything I want to share with everyone and give them a fruitful journey. Make it happen; life is beautiful, and so is the Universe. Where you live, with all the amenities, why do people suffer? I could only realise the fear in them. That fear has to be taken out of their system. I teach them how to look after life, beautiful manual, for everyone's, who they come to you and I show them the Pathway, and that is how my purpose has become very, very strong to reach out to everyone.

As I grew up during my school days, I became a member of Rotaract, and with Rotaract, I got to go to Dharavi, the slum area. One of the most significant slum areas on the Indian map is Bombay, and there, I had the opportunity to work with the people who lived there. Later on, after graduating from college, I became the secretary of The Society Of Helpers Of Mary. The sister I worked with took me under her wing, and with her, I was exposed to so many difficult situations, and this is where I came to know how people suffer and what solace she gives everyone. There are methods to provide for them. One night it was pouring rain, and we had to walk through dirty water to a family. The lady was due to have her delivery.

Though she had three children in the age group of five, six, and seven, they all were sitting on a stool even though the house was flooded with water. The lady was due to deliver, but there was not a single bedsheet that she could offer for the delivery. I was assisting sister Daya, and as I was helping, I had to prepare the methergine injection, the hot water to be used, and the umbilical cord being cut. There were no clothes to tie that; Sister Daya took her veil and tied it with it. She tore her blanket and gauze to disconnect the umbilical cord and my dupatta to wrap the child. That day, I realised what poverty is. How much do people suffer, why do they suffer, and what is the course of it? When the Universe has ample to give us, we provide everything to use, but we are unaware. This hit me hard; from that day onward, my journey was in a different direction. When people wanted their dreams fulfilled with material things, I used to communicate to the sky and hold it beautifully to know what it is that people don't see it. Why are they suffering so much? I wanted to curtail this suffering; that became my life's purpose.

When she worked a t Society of Helpers of Mary, one night, a woman walked in with a two-year-old and said she needed to go to the hospital and left her baby with Manjoo. In the middle of the night, Manjoo took the baby in because the lady said her only alternative was to leave the baby on the railway tracks. The following day when the sisters saw her, they asked her for papers, and all Manjoo could say was that there was no one to ask, so she took the baby in. Manjoo kept the little boy for two years until one day, the police came to her door with the mother demanding the child. Luckily when the police saw Manjoo, they recognised her and knew she was from the Helpers of sister Mary. The little boy was adopted in Germany, where he lives today, and is a successful engineer.

I was married, and I had my family. Over here, the purpose was very different, to assist them, guide them, to fulfil their needs and requirements. I ran the family's show, met everybody's needs, and took care of many challenges I had to endure. But there was somewhere a vacuum. I could always relate. And I could attend to everyone's need, whether it was an animal. I could understand their needs and requirements, whether a bird or a human being. This propelled me in the length and breadth to go ahead with the journey, and I could understand. I could relate to so many things they were unaware of.

Today at 72 years of age, I'll live my purpose. My day starts at 4:30 to 5:00 am with Praan Kriya, where I rejuvenate every cell of my body through yoga meditation. And then my havan. Havan is a ritual where you ignite a fire with auspicious ingredients of ghee wood and Chandan etc. I feel blessed. Besides this, I have exceptional children. Who, I teach dance and organise the program for them. I also have a visually challenged orchestra group. I contain shows for them; I have adopted a village at Alibaugh where during monsoon, we plant fruit trees in each and everyone's plot. So, this village has 11 to 12 varieties of fruits—fruit-yielding trees. And my number is 108 trees. It can be multiple of that. Today Manjoo plants fruit trees in all her neighboring villages to ensure that the children always have something to eat. Her childhood passion for eradicating poverty is her passionate purpose. She uses Feng Shui to assist people with health, wealth, and relationships and has many successful results. She is living her goal every day and making a difference in all the lives she touches.

My idea is to provide food to children, older adults, and birds. My feng shui demands a clutter-free house. Premises, I noticed, children outgrow grows their clothes, shoes, toys, and music systems. Either they have moved out of the house, or things are lying around. These old, I collect and distribute in the village sometimes. Also, I receive Furniture and curtains utensils. I bridge the gap between haves and have-nots. Feng Shui has opened a gateway to unlocking the harmonious energy for everyone.

**Manju Kar**

An initiative of Mental Resilience Mastery © 2022

## EMBRACING MY PASSION

My purpose is to serve all with love. I help connect with the Supreme through yoga, pranayama, prayers, and meditation. I encourage myself to experience life in all its glory and face my challenges with a sense of humour. I believe in being fearless in my pursuit to follow my heart. I am enthusiastic about being the catalyst that reminds people of their inner strength, beauty, and unique gifts. I strive to create safe spaces for people to connect and explore possibilities.

I am born in South Africa and live in the spirit of ubuntu (the concept of treating everybody with compassion, kindness, and humbleness). I have three exceptional children and a loving husband. I am an ICF-certified Life Coach. I have practised as a voluntary hospice counsellor, a Pranic healer, a Reiki Master, and a spiritual counsellor with an Honours Degree in Psychology. I am the author of the self-empowerment book *Rise Like a Phoenix.*

Self-development is my passion.
Curiosity about human psychology drives me.

An initiative of Mental Resilience Mastery © 2022

I am an avid yogi, meditator, and ferocious reader. I love to dance in the rain and find the positive side of the equation in all my experiences. My mission is to empower people to uncover their unique gifts and find joy by breaking all the shackles of conditioning. I am passionately pursuing my mission to empower one hundred thousand people of all ages to gain clarity and get unstuck to pursue their dreams within the next three years. It is time to stop negative self-talk, self-blame, and the feeling of never being good enough and take action to create the best and most authentic version of you ever!

I have not always been aware of my purpose. The ability to help people has always come naturally to me. When a neighbour had a physical ache, I was always on call to massage them to ease the pain. I was always there when people needed me to confide in or resolve their dilemmas. I never thought of it as my calling. Instead, I worked in the financial services sector for ten years. When you follow your purpose, you do so on a leap of faith, knowing that you are obeying your inner calling. Yes, it is risky because you do not see what the outcome will be. Many will be present to deter you. Not because they do not want you to succeed, but because they want to keep you safe and protected.The inner calling, however, is so strong that you either follow your heart or find yourself facing obstacle after obstacle. My challenge came as a blood clot landed me in hospital for two weeks.

I had been working twelve hours a day under stressful circumstances.
My body was telling me to stop.
I needed to change direction and follow my calling.

Although I loved the financial services world, I realised that my passion was to listen to people and empower them by showing them their strengths. I left the corporate world, pursued my love for healing, and studied different healing modalities and Psychology. At this point in our life, my husband and I were blessed with three beautiful children, and I dedicated my time to bringing up my family. My purpose changed to raising and nurturing my children. I completed my Honours in Psychology during this period of my life. I used my healing skills to do volunteer work for Hospice.

As a volunteer and healer, I was making a difference in people's lives; I felt an inner peace and knew I had found my purpose. Then the Pandemic stopped the world.

Everything I knew and was familiar with had changed. Simple things like meeting people became dangerous. You could not meet face-to-face or do the first-hand treatment. You could not visit the sick or the dying as you could be endangering their life. I had to reinvent myself. I asked myself, "How can I serve people effectively?" The world went digital. How do I take what I know and go digital? I found an opportunity to take all my knowledge and experience to serve more people through the digital world. Life coaching allows me to use all my knowledge and experience to be effective in people's lives. My purpose in action is to help people simplify and thrive.

Human beings can do anything they set their mind to. Through various stages of life, your purpose changes and becomes more defined. You may have remarkable success in all aspects of your life, but there comes a time when no matter how much you have acquired, there is a feeling of dissatisfaction or unfulfillment.

The ultimate purpose of one's life is to serve. The heart is set free by contribution and service, and joy abounds. Service can be in any form or deed that resonates with you as an individual. Surrounding yourself with people who push and inspire you is vital to succeeding. I have been blessed to be surrounded by people who have inspired me to pursue my passion.

My role model was my mother. She taught me that to have mental resilience, a good routine that encompasses spiritual practice like yoga, meditation, and prayers will keep me strong in challenging situations. Her purpose was also to serve. She started her young life in India, helped her mother in the fields, and did the family. The family was always her priority. However, she permanently extended her assistance to all members of the community. She would help families by caring for the children or helping with food when required. A fantastic woman, a single parent, bringing up three daughters. I leant from my mother that when you follow your purpose, you never take action to receive anything in return; you are guided by something much more substantial, love.

Another one of my heroes was my dear friend, who led by example and demonstrated love through action -**An Angel who graced our lives for too short a period.**
Her purpose was to serve, and she walked her talk. As a Sai devotee, she was always

undertaking assignments of service with a smile. Nothing was too much to manage. She went through chemotherapy multiple times and endured it with a smile. She always had a kind word of encouragement for fellow patients. She never complained of pain once, even though you could see it in her eyes. Every year she did a stationary collection for the school children that needed it. When natural disasters hit the country, she would always be involved in collecting essentials for those affected. She started groups to support people who were struggling. She started a movement to educate people on how to create less waste and save the earth .in the community. She is an incredible lady who pursued her purpose till her final days on earth. I feel so blessed to have been touched by her friendship. She showed me that there are so many opportunities to serve. I just needed to seize them.

When you are in tune with your purpose you are more creative and open to experiences. You continuously get out of your comfort zone because your need to make a difference is vital. People are pursuing their purpose in many different ways:
- Providing for their families and nurturing the next generation

- Pursuing their sports or career goals
- Being a mentor
- Shaping the world for a better future

Never underestimate your contribution. Never overestimate what is required to serve your purpose. Do what you do well to make a change.

Discovering my purpose has clarified how I may serve humanity using my skills and knowledge. I have met many people who are so conditioned and busy being everything for someone else that they have lost sight of who they are. They continue to play a secondary role to their spouses or family members. To conform, to fit in, to be acceptable and be a people pleaser. No more! You were born with greatness, and it is time to break free. The time has come for you to embrace yourself as you are because, yes, you are unique, you are precious, and you are enough. My purpose is to remind you by demolishing your limiting beliefs and redirecting you towards your dreams and desires. As a life coach, I fulfil my goal by sharing tools with people to get unstuck and thrive. When you know your purpose in life, you begin to lead the life you were destined to lead.

**Pretiksha Diar:**
**https://linktr.ee/pretikshadiar.**

## FOUR WORDS THAT CHANGED MY LIFE

"Having a purpose is the difference between making a living and making a life."

-Tom Thiss

"There is no greater gift you can give or receive than to honour your calling. It's why you were born. And how you became most truly alive."

-Oprah Winfrey

"If you can't figure out your purpose, figure out your passion. For your passion will lead you right into your purpose."

-Bishop T.D. Jakes

Some find their purpose easily early in life; some take years and go through many changes before narrowing down to what they deeply vibe with to make it their vision and mission.

In my journey, my focus has changed inward to outward and vice versa until I could concise my purpose in "Four Words That Changed My Life:"

**"Learn – Share – Show – Grow" (L-S-S-G.)**

An initiative of Mental Resilience Mastery © 2022

It seems simple; however, if you give it a good thought, it's the basic seeded from early childhood, entrenched in the Montessori School of teaching.

You Learn from your five senses. So, learning is continuous every moment of your life. "The day you stop learning is the day you die."

-My Grandma

Our teacher took pains to Share knowledge with love, care, and patience. Some of us were quick learners, while others took time. She has patiently handheld to Show the way to overcome challenges faced. That helped all students to Grow their knowledge and learning of life. The teacher gained precious experience and developed personally.

I am writing for you at 70; however, I take you back to 6 decades where my intention took root. Besides my teachers, I was blessed to have very spiritually evolved grandparents who could manifest whatever they wished for with their Power of Positive Thinking – not the way people know it today. This was deep and powerful, like surrendering an intent to the Universe and then being one with the

Universe to tap into the Universal Energy Force of creation.

Allow me to share one story and visualize it as I go.

My grandma had a picture of a beautiful little girl with golden hair and blue eyes peeping from behind a tree, showing herself up to her waist. During one of my grandma's pregnancies, she desired a child exactly like that and kept looking at the picture and seeding her intent. Everyone, especially grandpa, teased her and asked where she would get the genes. To make a long story short, she gave birth to a carbon copy of that picture – same features, golden hair, blue eyes. However, the child died within an hour as it had developed only till the waist.

My grandma always narrated this story to teach us 'how to ask' even from the Universe. It would be best if you were as specific as you can be and asked for qualities of what you want without comparing with anything or anybody. Specify what you want, when, and how much, and give minute details. Yet not attaching to the results. Seed your intent and surrender to the Universe with full faith. This was significant learning for me.

Being a person with helper traits, I have always shared my love and time to help and support others. I naturally look for the good in others, and when I admire something about someone, I reach out and say so. I genuinely praise and generously share my time, energy, attention, and affection. My focus was outward from childhood, making a difference in people's lives.

In grade 9, a girl, Shirin, was stuck in that grade and was finding it difficult to move forward. She was tall, beautiful, big, and much older than her classmates. She came from an economically challenged and uneducated family. She had given up on life itself. I decided to take up the challenge. I talked to my mother about her. My mother was an embodiment of abundant love. She gave me extra food, and I started to share my food with her during school breaks and befriended her. I worked on first developing her faith and belief in herself that she could pass not only grade 9 but grade 10 too and graduate from school to get her certification. Then every break after eating, coming earlier in the morning, helping her on holidays, I tutored her with the basics of each subject, bit by bit, in a way she could understand and grasp. I also reached out to my teachers to ask her simple questions she could answer to boost her confidence. Viola! I could visualize a creation of a new individual – her walk changed, she stopped stooping, she had the most beautiful smile on her face, and her friends, instead of teasing her, talked to her and included her in conversations and games. Shirin passed grade 9 and was promoted with her classmates to grade 10 – a very eventful day of her life. She showered me with gratitude and blessings that brought tears to my eyes (even as I write, reliving those memories).

My challenge doubled in grade 10. It meant a year of hard work as I wanted to take up science in college and needed a higher percentage. However, the joy of seeing her graduate with us was worth every ounce of effort from both of us. Sheer bliss! I was happier with her result than mine though I was one of the toppers. Shirin will always hold a special place in my heart and me in hers. She lights up like a candle whenever she sees me, even today. I think her blessings have helped me in my life's journey.

You must be wondering how sharing these stories is related to my purpose. Well, it is. As I mentioned at the start, my focus now changed from outward to inward. As I grew older and had a family, it changed from being there for others to being there for myself and every family member. I believe "Charity begins at home." I had my mother-in-law and my ageing mother-in-law's mother-in-law too, my father-in-law having health challenges, my parents, younger siblings, my husband, and my one and only daughter, the love of my life. I was balancing my family and my career. As I supported my husband in his career and health challenges, I stood by him like a rock.

Later in my career, when my daughter was independent, I was Director of a College, and my focus changed again towards helping my students and staff "Live Life at Level 10." I also started social work for senior citizens.

My daughter settled in Melbourne, Australia, and had a family of her own. As my grandchildren grew, my focus shifted back inwards towards my core family. As I was introspecting on my purpose, it dawned on me that I need to "Be the change I desire!' I realized you could only give what you have. So, I worked on raising my vibes to higher frequencies within and in my immediate environment. As I meditated, tapping into my Spirit, I evolved the magical four words that gave clarity to my purpose – "Learn, Share, Show, Grow."

Henceforth, I am looking forward to reaching out into the world. The Pandemic has made us more aware, now than ever, that millions of people need love, care, and support. I intend to actively reach out to help people, especially senior citizens who struggle in life to fend for themselves and feel lonely even if they are living with their families.

I intend to share love and make others feel loved so they can share it further into the world.

## Who Am I?

I am **NAWAZ MARKER** from Mumbai, currently living in Australia. A Coach who endeavors to make a positive difference in people's lives!
A speaker with a "Limitless ME" Mastermind to help seniors retain their glory even as the years pass by and remain happy, healthy, peaceful, and prosperous till the end.

**A Networker with Enagic Kangen Water to ensure good health for the entire family.**

An initiative of Mental Resilience Mastery © 2022

26years in my Avon business, empowering women financially, emotionally, and mentally. Experiences of my 35 years of a beautiful relationship with my mother-in-law I have shared in my book - "7 Sweet Maneuvers To Bond With Your Mother-In-Law." I also have Co-Authored three other books till today.

I am an NLP Practitioner, with my certificate signed by Richard Bandler, Co-Founder of NLP.

I am a Reiki & Ho'Oponopono Healer.

I am a Science Graduate from Bombay University & have done Systems Management from NIIT. I later worked with them and had an opportunity to be instrumental in starting the computerization of banking in India.

I have years of experience in the Corporate HR sector in Senior Management & for my last assignment, I was Director of Nirmala Niketan Polytechnic college, where I guided students and staff to "Live Life at Level 10".

I am multi-talented - a graceful and energetic dancer, passionate about doing creative work like stained glass, metal embossing, ceramics, mural art, etc., and creating new things out of the old. These are my buzz moments where I experience the great joy of being one with creation.

I am also an adventurous person who, on her 25th Anniversary, went scuba diving 22ft in Cairns, the highest bungee jump on the Gold Coast, and sky diving from 12,000 ft in Sydney.

I am abundant in unconditional love. I believe:
"You can overcome any challenge and obstacle with love."
"Whatever happens, happens for the best."

Being a Coach, I have helped people transform from being a victim to being a victor, experiencing breakthroughs in their lives.

I am an International Speaker and conduct my Mastermind, "Limitless ME", allowing all to live life at their full potential.

My vision is to help 1000 people by the end of 2025 and empower their lives, especially seniors. I aim to achieve this with my mission and purpose of sharing my learnings, showing people the path, by helping them grow personally and achieve success in their lives. I have and follow a time-tested 10-week system that works every time for all situations. I also have my healing programs.

An initiative of Mental Resilience Mastery © 2022

I wish the world would celebrate my 100th birthday.

To know more about me, a woman with a chronological age of 70, yet emotional, energy, and mental age of 17, check me out
**Nawaz Marker at:**
https://linktr.ee/nawazmarkercoach.

## CHANGE YOUR STORY, CHANGE YOUR

## LIFE

What gives meaning to my life?
I was the first-born, most loved daughter.
I was my papa's princess.
We were four sisters showered with unconditional love.
My parents lived a simple life of contribution to the world. Every birthday we meet some children and have meals and sweets with them. My dad, a scientist from BARC, showed us how spirituality was entwined in science. They adored each other so much. They were the epitome of love and respect for each other.
I grew up in an atmosphere of smiles, laughter and hugs.
Everything was abundant.
Unconditional love, gratitude, happiness, contribution, kindness and above all, there was a connection to Divinity. The Tag line at home was Be like water, love like water. I was free flowing, singing and dancing girl, just like water.
My mom's eyes were sparkling, her face was always glowing, and her hands were always GIVING. My dad is ALWAYS shining.

One day I met a young, thin, shy, simple boy in an examination hall. He was calm and serene. The exam hall was buzzing with anxiety, but this boy was so quiet. Slowly we became friends forever, and one fine day, we tied the knot.

I tried a lot to please everyone, to fit in. Rejection was the only response. I started singing a 'blame' song in my head. I don't believe that it's my fault. What wrong have I done? I was angry, very angry.

My dad one day sat me down and told me, "You can keep whining, blame your destiny or you can FORGIVE them and move forward". ACCEPTANCE of this situation first and then taking action was the key. I was grateful that my husband was supporting me.

As my mindset shifted, the Universe had lovely plans for me. I got an invitation to make a home for ourselves. I said YES. I didn't know how that would happen with a Joint SALARY OF Rs 2200/- pm. Even the loan givers disagreed.

I found a business card one day, a masterstroke from the Universe that belonged to the chairman of ICICI bank. We went to see him, and he sanctioned our loan to be repaid in 20 years. The idea was to have a bare minimum of instalments.

Someone out there in the cosmos is looking for you, offering abundance to you. We must tune into it, align with it, and receive it.

So then I was unstoppable. I had to make this house into my home sweet home. In 1984, We booked our place, which was under construction. We entered our home in 1990 with two infants, one in my arms and the other in my husband's arms. We carried a hand-pumping stove, four plates, four spoons, four cups, and zero furniture. But with a lot of hope, Faith, determination, love in our hearts, brilliance in our eyes, and a deep connection with Divinity.

My purpose was to stand on my feet on my own. I didn't want to trouble my parents or my in-laws. I never dreamt of becoming a considerable doctor but a caring doctor who could give hope and empathy to her patients.

Because my WHY was so strong, nothing seemed difficult. Both of us worked day and night. Soon I left my job to start my dental clinic in 1991. It was a tiny 7 feet by 7 feet cubicle. It was too small. So this again helped. I applied for a loan for my clinic premises.

I took loans for my car, laboratory equipment, furniture and many more. My in-laws visited our house, and they were proud of us. Loans helped us value money, and we worked hard to repay our instalments. Wastage of expenses on unnecessary entertainment was not at all on the cards. At this time, books came to my rescue. Books have always been my best friend; reading made me wiser and helped my children.

Now it was my turn to build my children. Like my dad gave me the environment to bloom and blossom. That's what I did. I always wanted to be a good parent and a great partner, like my dad.

I was always seeking something.

To become a happy person.

 My songs changed.

One day I was invited to a workshop on Yoga, and I was so enamoured that I enrolled on the Teacher's training course in Yoga the next day. To understand myself better, I registered for some classes, one after the other.

I soon became a Certified Yoga Teacher and an NLP practitioner. I did my advanced counselling course and became Louise Hay's "Heal Your Life" facilitator. I started teaching Yoga, Breathing, and Meditation to one and all. I applied all my knowledge to counsel my patients, and when I conducted HYL workshops, listening to the stories of so many people, I changed.

This was my calling. Every day, bit by bit, my life was changing.

My husband and I were improving in our clinical practice.

Listening to each of my patients, I surveyed and researched and concluded that the happy people were healthier and more productive. I reconfirmed my belief that "Happy living is healthy Living". This became my mantra. I started spreading this message everywhere.

As they saw us working so hard, our children were building us. Both my boys have been a pillar of strength for us.

I grew daily, moment by moment, into an influential person.

I was always seeking something.

That something is seeking me.

One day, my mom felt weak while doing her routine activities. This was the beginning of a disaster in my life. I lost her in one month. A woman who never took paracetamol in her life just left this world in a second.

My dad followed suit.

He could not survive without her.

I lost both my parents, one after the other. My parents had stood by me, and the spiritual seeds in me since childhood made me surrender to God. I felt LOST.

During the grief, the Universe came to my rescue; introduced me to a 'senior citizens' group which has been my pillar of strength till today. They showered me with so much LOVE.

At this time, I wrote my book "Shukriya Zindagi". The memories of my wonderful

childhood were flashing in my brain. My parents were my role models, my first teachers. They sacrificed a lot to give me a great life filled with unconditional love, value systems, discipline, and spirituality.
I started writing.
Writing helped me to rediscover myself.
I met myself.
A new Alka was born.
I started singing and dancing again, and my happiness knew no bounds.
At age 60, I participated in a dance competition, a turning point in my life. I learned a lot. The backstage showed me that we all have to practice our script. No matter what goes wrong, the show must go on. Coming out of my comfort zone was the only way to success. PRACTICE made my dance steps perfect, and I won a big prize.
I started my masterclass "The Magic of believing in Myself" this time. All youngsters were also invited, and this became a hit.
I was so much happier with my new mindset. I wanted to spread this happiness to everyone. At that time, I started my course, "Life begins at 60", and Punjab National Bank invited me to take sessions for retirees. In my Happiness School, I show everyone how easy it is to be happy. No one is responsible for our happiness.

An initiative of Mental Resilience Mastery © 2022

Neuroscience shows us the way. When we focus on happiness, peace, love and gratitude, our brain activates that pathway. When we focus on what we want, that's what we get. When we stop complaining about fault finding, we attract happiness.

Excuses, blaming, and grumbling makes us powerless. When we take responsibility for our actions, can we be happy? Changing my perspective towards life was all that the d our viewpoint. This helps us to see life with new eyes. During the Pandemic, I became an IYCT coach, now on an incredible journey.

We are all storytellers. The way we tell our stories is the way we believe them. When we change our narration, we can change our stories and lives. We can live as if nothing is a miracle or everything is a miracle.

The Universe has always helped me. I am at a great place in my life right now. I am happy. I am grateful. I am moving forward. I am helping everyone. I love everyone. "Love is the essence of life". This, incidentally, is also my masterclass.

We can live as if everything is a miracle or nothing is a miracle. Imagine a life where nothing will go wrong. The power is in us. We can create the life we want, a beautiful, wonderful life, the successful life of our dreams, a life of fulfilment, a life of contentment.

**Dr Alka Chadha:**
https://linktr.ee/alkachadha

## THE WIRELESS CONNECTION OF

## THOUGHTS

**"Every strong woman had only one choice! To be a victim or a hero? Write your own script. It will be worth reading, inspiring, and healing all."**

**- Jyoti Gidwani**

My purpose is to help women and children(families) acknowledge their self-worth, get clarity about their goals and desires through vision boards and manifestation meditations and know about their inner powers. We can develop spiritual muscles by scientifically understanding the role of the brain, heart, and mind by tuning into cosmic frequency through meditation, with faith, by surrendering and taking actions to see the desired goal crystalise within the desired time frame.

With 27 years of journey as a manifesto, I have experienced many breakthroughs and insights and received beautiful testimonials from various participants.

An initiative of Mental Resilience Mastery © 2022

I did my schooling at Scindia School Gwalior, one of the best schools in India, and Engineering from Pune university. As I grew up, I became a shy and introverted personality with dreams buried in my eyes, words hoarded in my throat and feelings stuffed in deep corners. I wanted to break open the shell!

After getting married, I entered another dimension by reading books from my husband's collection. You can call it synchronicity, my journey as a manifestor began. Intrigued by life, energy, soul, and spirituality since childhood, I completed Yoga TTC, authored my first book on yoga in 1998 and dedicated it to my Guruji as my service.

It has been in print for the last 25 years.
I studied several healing modalities like Acupressure, Reiki, Mind control, Feng shui, Astrology, and Vastu Shastra.
Motherhood opened new horizons for me.

For the past ten years, I have been in the field of education. Life coaching was another dream locked in the safe vault of my eyes until almost two decades later; finally, I met my mentor, whom I had seen in a BBC documentary.

**My story**

The wireless connection of thoughts is about my real-life journey and experience of transcendence. I had my first miscarriage two years after marriage. Then came long periods of testing times, trying different treatments and therapies and bowing down at every spiritual place and endless prayers. An extended period of unending patience and perseverance. After fourteen years of testing and multiple miscarriages, finally, God heard our prayers, and I conceived in the first attempt of IVF. All went well; we even registered the hospital room according to the due date of delivery given by the doctor. Alas! Fate took another turn. A subsequent shock of mid-term pregnancy loss came as if that much suffering was not sufficient. The unbearable grief left me devastated and shattered. Unable to manage the grief after a string of losses, life seemed meaningless. I had to smile and continue with my duties, but inside, my heart bled because of unseen, unhealed, and unacknowledged wounds. It was like living with two identities, one coping with unbearable pain and the other pretending to be all right. A fragment of my soul had left with my little angel, and the remaining had to live for near and dear ones on earth.

The period of grief is a very tormenting phase. They say time heals everything. That was not true for me. Was it depression? No way! Can a woman afford to get depressed? I do not know! The word depression wasn't in our vocabulary. I knew I had to take charge and get out of this low state without any external help. I have always believed that all answers are within, and I knew I had to dive deeper to find mine.

The fact is, I had to take a step to heal myself as I could not bear the pain of my loved ones around me, who could see my internal wounds like an MRI Machine. I recharged my battery by meditating, reading scriptures, and praying. One by one, mentors appeared, and all pieces of the puzzle fell in place.

Each one of us must deal with grief at some point in life. The vacuum cannot be explained. Grief takes a lifetime to heal. How do you recover when you have lost a piece of your heart and soul? The most difficult days are birthdays and anniversaries. In my case, it was three days – the day of conception, miscarriage, and due date of delivery.

Grief is experienced in the form of a sudden tsunami triggered by an earthquake of thoughts, memories, feelings, emotions, songs or words. The most dangerous part is that one gets addicted to pain without realising it. Pain is energy, and energy can be transformed. I knew I had to change this pain into power before it started melting and eating me up from the inside. I chose the path of a wounded hero rather than a self-pity victim.

I prayed for the soul to return to me on my pre-selected date. Yes, indeed, my prayers were answered! My manifestation came true – my child was in my arms on my selected date. I looked up and said, "thank you God – I knew it was you!"
This journey brought me to this realisation and breakthrough that thoughts can travel to the world beyond our senses, to the unseen divine world. Not only is someone up there listening, but they also fulfilled my request by providing evidence!

Knowing that the Supreme Power had been addressing my thoughts and answering my prayer helped me re-establish my faith. This insight and breakthrough also brought in a comforting feeling that our loved ones who leave us and go away to the unseen, unreachable world can still be connected through our **Personal Wi-Fi on our own Thoughts-App.**

In India, we know how our great saints, seers, and gurus connected with the universe telepathically with their super powers (biological Wi-Fi) through thoughts. How many of you have experienced that we remember someone, and the next moment we receive a phone call from that person?

The Pineal gland is the cosmic antenna. The brain is like a transmitter and a receiver. It can send and receive signals through time, space, and dimensions.
Writing heals. It is like meditation. During one such tidal tsunami of grief, when I had lost my maternal uncle, my pain just spilt onto paper, giving words to my dismay. I want to share my poem "Little Monica" with you all. I use it as a means to heal the grief that consumes us.

## Little Monica

Little Monica looked out of the Window…
Oh! How badly she missed her mom,
Without her, there was complete silence at home!
She remembered her mother's stories and words,

The Moon is the link that connects us to
God's world!
 Her mother had once told her when our
loved ones leave,
We feel overwhelmed; we want to cry in
grief!
Pour your heart out to the moon,
Like 5G, our messages to the other world
will reach very soon!

Her eyes were teary,
Her soul longed for love, was tired and
weary!
But she was at least sure of one thing,
That moon was always listening!

This was her private hot-line to Mom,
Which offered only one-way
communication!
Ever since mom had gone, she would wave
to the Moon every night,
And suggest upgrading the app from only
incoming to Video chat!


Technology has been changing so fast,
From landlines to mobiles to video chat!
What stops God from upgrading the
application?
So that with our loved ones, face to face,
we can have live communication!

An initiative of Mental Resilience Mastery © 2022

Before Little Monica went to bed, she looked out of her window,
Now warmth of mom's hug was provided by her pillow!
Seeing the moon so up-close and near,
She felt as if the moon was responding to her!

Even though she stretched but could not reach,
Moon linked her to 'Mama'; that is what her mom would teach!
**The mind can reach anywhere in fractions of a second,**
**Only loving thoughts can transcend the realms and get to the other end!**

Jyoti Gidwani

**Vision**: My vision is to awaken and empower women and children. Awakened and empowered women raise an empowered next generation.

**Mission**: My mission is to help people see their potential, live their lives to the fullest by instilling a mindset shift, and achieve balance and success in all aspects of life.

If you resonate with my vision and mission and are ready to transform towards a happy, healthy, abundant, and joyful life, I welcome you to my tribe. Together we can

An initiative of Mental Resilience Mastery © 2022

awaken and empower one soul, one family at a time and transform the world into a beautiful place.

**"Same divine force that created the sun, moon, planets and galaxies made You!**
**The cosmic energy is continuously charging our body which houses the soul.**
**You do matter in this universe!**
**You are here for a purpose.**
**Have you found yours yet?**

**Jyoti Gidwani–**
**https://linktr.ee/jyoti.gidwani**

An initiative of Mental Resilience Mastery © 2022

## FROM POWERLESS TO JOYFULNESS

## AND FREEDOM

We are empowering people to love themselves and find their self-worth.

One little girl, Akanksha, was born into a joint family. The eldest child of the family, moreover, you can say the girl child. From childhood, I was taught that I am a girl and that I need to sacrifice many things for the family; your wishes should not be your priority and are unnecessary. I was asked to live for the people around me, listen to them, do what they like and keep people happy around me. These things are going to bring happiness to your life.

When I was in class 5th, around ten years old, I was told you are grown up; you need to learn household chores as, after all, you are going to get married, and these things are essential. I was not allowed to play outside and play with kids as we were seven kids in the family; my sister and my cousin's brother are almost the same age, and the difference is less than a year as I was the eldest daughter in the family. All the burden of becoming a good wife and daughter-in-law was on me. As if I play outside, what will happen?

Since then, I have buried all my wishes and desire in my heart and my thinking. I was a good player; I used to play cricket and badminton. I am still a suitable blower and great at high jumping. I wanted to dance and learn Kathak, but everyone thought it was a waste of time and no use. So, I learnt Kathak as much as I could learn in school hobby class.

I was a shy kid, but now I have become more introverted and never demanded what I wanted, even if it was genuine. I used to remain silent. I was happy when people around me werc happy. And I started living as people around me wanted to live. Believing what they told me about myself and what was good for me, I used to wear what they liked, talk as they wanted me, did what they wanted me to do.

Slowly, Slowly I started moving away from the people. I started living in the home, enjoying television, school studies and household work. I did not enjoy going out and meeting people. I got 1-2 friends, but after a long friendship, I broke it as I felt terrible about it. I thought I was used and didn't have self-worth; I only lived for her good. We have been friends since school and in my engineering also.

I was thrilled in my last year of engineering because I felt free. I got placed in a good company. It was all excellent. I was enjoying my success in getting a job, but it did not last for long. Everyone started planning and seeing boys for my marriage, so I was not allowed to join the job; I was just 22 years old. But then, I wanted to move out of home and see the world, explore it, experience it and live an independent life. But I could not.

Searching for a good boy and a good family took 1.5 years until I decided to do an MBA and pass the entrance exam. As I was happy this time in my PG, I thought I would enjoy it to the fullest; I was thrilled. But how can I be satisfied as I have to learn many lessons from life?

My family liked the alliance, and I did not find any points about the person to reject. So, it was decided that I would complete my MBA after marriage and from Indore only, and my husband was working in Pune. I asked my husband once if I could choose Pune college, but no, I was in-laws' home.

Here also, I was carrying out the same emotion and situation. I was asked to obey them. To fulfil their wishes even though I am not skilled for it. I was taunted, suppressed and disrespected. I allowed them to do this all. I was physically, mentally, and emotionally weak, and everything was inside me. There was no one to understand me. As I wanted to complete my MBA, I ignored everything that filled me. I tried the best possible things I could do for my in-laws' and the home. But as I was not confident and empowered. I always felt suppressed; they used, blamed me, and never respected me as a person.

Life was trying to teach me a lesson. But I could not understand until I became a mother. I realised then where am I heading in my life and what am I doing to my life. I felt as if my daughter gave me rebirth as a person, as a human being. The energy that I am living, I can't give this life to my daughter. But how, I thought to fulfil my desire to be independent. For mine and my daughter's betterment.

I started working in a company in Pune as my daughter started going to school. I enjoyed the phase of my life as an independent person. But still, something was bothering me, and I did not know. Now, what was in my life about to change? My husband planned to start a business in the home town, and we were again back to Indore with my in-laws', and now there was the sister-in-law, who was and is a very dominating person. The feeling of unworthiness was so high that I felt that in my family, everything would revolve around her only. I, as a family member, was not taken into account. I was jobless now, my daughter and I were not welcomed in the house, and we were not respected as the person. The blame game and not doing anything for my family was totally on me; no one bothered me whether I had a fever103-degree Fahrenheit.

I was struggling in my life to live with my mother-in-law and sister-in-law. My husband had no time for me; he was just busy starting the business—so much negativity filled me. The feeling of being unloved, unworthy, and useless surrounded me and impacted my daughter. I fought for myself, but this did not work; I wanted to leave that house, but where to go?

I started my playschool for kids, but it did not work out as I carried a heavy burden of going out and working, although I cooked food, did pooja, cleaned the house, and ironed the clothes. I took my daughter to my playschool, and not a single day was I allowed to leave her at home. I have constantly been taunted, and

I accepted it. I was filled with guilt. I closed it within a year only.

I decided to work on myself. I started seeing someone who could understand and guide me to change me. And something you wish full-heartedly and with pure intention comes to you. I was looking for the coaching program but online as I had one year daughter, so I could not leave her. I prayed online, and covid started, which changed my life for the better. I got the excellent program that is coaching program, Coach to Fortune. This program has changed my life entirely for the better me.

I started my journey of finding myself, loving myself, and having self-worth. I realised that I have the power to make my future and leave a legacy for my two beautiful daughters. Now things started falling into place. My life has become attractive. I have transformed from within.

Now I know to live life by saying –"Live the life that I want to live not what the others want you to live."

Now, as I am empowered in my life, I found my self-worth. I started loving myself. Now I understood what was going wrong in my life. You know something that now things have changed completely. My attitude towards life has changed. Now I think of changing the situation by changing myself and taking responsibility. Now my priority is changed for the better me.

I suffered a lot, which impacted my life in every area, like physically, in relationships, career, fun and recreation, with friends and so on.
I would love to reach out to the people stuck in life and unable to understand what's happening.

Each of us needs to understand our worth; we need to love ourselves and realise that there is nothing wrong with doing what we like to do. Build and live the life you desire for. As humans, we must understand that we are the best of ourselves. To be healthy, happy, and at peace, we need to be clear and firm, stand and speak for ourselves, and find our truth.

Now, I am on the path of empowering people for their betterment. I want to assign 50 lakhs people in my remaining life span.
I found my life's purpose, and now I want to reach out to people and help them find their purpose in life.

I am a Motivate to Empower People Coach – Akanksha Inani  Kabra (Coach AKS – The Reflection of Life). I have started my YouTube Channel, am the author of a book and designing my program with my life experience.

**Akansha:**
https://linktr.ee/akankshainanikabra

An initiative of Mental Resilience Mastery © 2022

## BE JOYFUL AND FREE YOU!

MY PURPOSE is to live joyfulness and freedom from physical, emotional, mental, and spiritual challenges and to impact and transform one million lives to live a life of delight and privilege. This also means that I would specifically help women to re-establish their *identity* and grab back their *power* to lead joyfully free lives.

My name is Dr. Parvin Lasania. I am a medical doctor, a counselling psychologist, and a life coach living this *incredible lifestyle of joyfulness and freedom* today. I help people re-discover themselves, their strengths, values, goals, and their heart's desires through awareness and self-love.

I am now enjoying a hale and healthy life which is energetic and full of productivity. I now feel strong not only in terms of physical health, sorted in the head and feel serene, calm, composed and gratified. I currently lead a fulfilled life with plenty of enjoyable moments every single day of my life. With my physical and emotional health being taken care of, I have become the most productive version of myself, doing the things I love to do. I have reached this stage in my life through a process that was not always like this.

1985-1990: Parvin is a cheerful, happy, bubbly, excited teenager. Topping in her school and colleges filled her with confidence. She is in love with her life and has lots of dreams in her eyes and ambitions for the future. Her heart sings with joy, and she feels free like a bird to pursue her life's goals of practising as a doctor and helping the world become a healthier and better place to live in.

The years 1995-2005: The once joyful teenager has now become a sad, depressed, angry and resentful person. She was mad at herself and everyone around her. She did not want to live anymore. Pulling through each day of her life is now drudgery for her. Every second day, she finds herself running a temperature or having a splitting headache. She could not eat well, sleep well, and did not have the energy to do anything for herself or her family. There were times when she spent the whole day lying in bed, unmotivated to do anything. This went on for quite some time, and one day, she got diagnosed with tuberculosis.

"What is the situation that is causing all this?" she asked herself. She was being insulted by the people around her; she was being criticised for how she looked and how she did whatever she did. She was compelled to follow orders and conform to the people around her. She was denied the right and freedom to decide for herself and choose what she wanted. She felt controlled and trapped. She thought that she could not be the person she was meant to be, the person she wanted to be. The constant chatter in her head resulted in her ill health, she realized years later. She was not feeling good inside, and it was a zero productive life that she was living, far from the life she had dreamt of and wanted for herself.

One day she questioned herself, "Am I going to live like this for the rest of my life till the day I die". "Am I going to end my life right now" because that was what she felt like doing? But she thought deeply and found the answer to both the questions. It was 'A BIG NO'. At this point, she decided to take responsibility for her own life and exercise the freedom to *choose* her own life's journey and to live the life she wanted and dreamt of having since her growing years.

Parvin decided to rebuild her *IDENTITY, REDESIGN* her life, and *BOUNCE BACK* according to her innermost values and beliefs. She chose to ignore the noises around her and to change the voices in her head. She understood that others' opinions of her does not decide her value. She realized that the ship never sank because of the water around it, but because of the water inside it.

The year 2005– The process of re-inventing herself started for her with SHARPENING THE SAW. She *decided* to take up new courses and nourish herself mentally and creatively. She did her master's in Counseling Psychology and took up several other short diploma courses to help her feel more empowered and better equipped to face the world. As part of her journey, she healed herself through a process. Once she recovered herself, she helped others get rid of their baggage. She worked as a Counselor helping children and teenagers with their challenges and helping them get a cutting edge in working towards excellence. She helped women and couples navigate through their differences and lead more harmonious lives in sync with each other and, in the process, enabled women to maintain and establish their identities.

The next decade 2010-2020: Parvin started loving herself more and more each day by taking care of her physical, mental, emotional, and spiritual health. Her secret formula was loving herself and which helped her in the following achievements:

• Physical health: She created a massive shift in her health by changing her lifestyle. A) Exercise- This became part of her daily life. Not exercising was not an option. A regular workout time got fixed. She got herself a Coach and allowed herself to be mentored. She communicated her goals to everyone at home and received their support. Time and space boundary she drew to move ahead in this area. B) Nutrition She made nutritional changes and ate healthily. All her meal plans were decided by her the previous day. She stopped adjusting and compromising with the ingredients and spent time shopping for and preparing her meals. She started eating proteins, vegetarian or non-vegetarian, at every meal. Vegetables in sufficient quantities became the given. Salads and soups became a part of her diet. Timings of her meals were maintained at every cost. She gave up on sugars and sweets. C) Water Drinking water in sufficient quantities and at regular intervals became a part of her lifestyle, and she worked on an auto-pilot. D) Sleep- Sleeping for sufficient hours and at a regular time was a challenge because of the schedule of the other members at home. But she overcame it by putting herself first, communicating her needs and goals, and being determined in her pursuit. E) Mind programming – "I am a fat-burning machine" was Parvin's new affirmation and mantra that she repeated throughout the day. She told herself that she could be the most energetic person that she wanted to be.

• Emotional health: Parvin attained her best version in this regard by A) Journaling and writing her autobiography. This resulted in increased self-awareness, healing as well as a transformation. She was able to reframe the things which were affecting her. B) Gratitude journaling every single day helped her to appreciate all the things she had in her life, which she did not give much
importance to and focus on. C) Doing small actions every day that made her happy, like dancing for a few minutes, playing with her son and growing vegetables on her rooftop garden, and listening to songs. D) Setting boundaries for those around her helped her prioritize herself. E) Having small daily, weekly, and monthly goals gave her a strong sense of fulfilment and achievement.

• Mental health: A) Communication: She changed her style from authoritarian to authoritative. B) She developed more empathy towards the people around her, C) More listening started happening D) More hugging and less tugging became the rule. E) Kindness was shown to the other family members. F) Forgiveness became a given for her daily. Lots of letting go were being practised. Giving all of the above to the others resulted in her getting them back in a double measure, even if it took some time.

• Spiritual health: A) Praying five times a day has helped me build up my Faith and Gratitude. It was a constant reminder that certain things are under our control and others beyond, and we must develop faith and trust in the creator and giver. B) Charity giving to people from whom I can't expect anything in return and who are unknown to me. C) Understanding and living by my values. I started working on Trust building, Perseverance, Commitment, Gratitude, Mindfulness, Love, and Achievement.

I, Dr Parvin, a medical doctor and a psychologist, honestly believe that Physical well-being is closely connected to mental, emotional, and spiritual well-being. Today after working on myself, I am free of all the health challenges I once faced, and I am no more on any medication. I now help people lead a life of holistic well-being by de-cluttering their minds and grabbing back their power to write their own stories.

**Dr Parvin:**
https ://linktr.ee/coachparvinlasania

## MY CORE-IN GIVING

**The Purpose:**
*To live my life to add values to people's lives so that they have a new meaning in life, a sense of fulfilment, a vision to live for, and experience transformation.*

**About The Author**
Prabhunath Pandey is a Freemason, an Environmentalist, a Quality & HR Consultant, a Six Sigma Black Belt, a Quality Lead Assessor, a Life & Career Coach, the Founder of Master Minds-Living a Balanced Life & Creating Value to Experience Transformation (CVET), a Crypto & NFT Investor & Advisor, and the Author of "Patience"- The Transformational Tool in the Wheel of Life.

**Why That Purpose**
After diving deep within myself, I connected at a very high level with the purpose I defined. Only after years of searching and emptiness could I relate to something limitless, empowering, and emotionally connecting. I am no longer feeling empty; I am ready to give and give and give.
I am now living my life intending to give, making a difference in people's lives, and

assisting them in achieving their goals using all the skills and knowledge I have acquired to date. This has become so simple because it is now aligned with my life's purpose.

**How I Got My Definite Purpose:**
**"If you have a strong purpose in life, you don't have to be pushed. Your passion will drive you there. "Roy T. Bennett**

The fundamental question that plagued me for nearly four decades following my engineering degree was linked to a single word: "Purpose".
What's the purpose of my life? What's the point of my existence? Who am I? What's mine? Why?
I had these questions, for which I didn't get an answer until June 2021.
The month and year are essential because it was around this time that I could find and define my purpose. After going through several grilling sessions, brainstorming sessions, and one-on-one interactions, this blew my mind.

**"The two most important days in life are the day you are born and the day you find out your why." – Mark Twain**

An initiative of Mental Resilience Mastery © 2022

Let me tell you a short anecdote before I share how I discovered my calling.

During one of the learning programs with one of the top coaches in India, there was an exercise on finding "your passion", and something struck me. I started connecting several dots; my reason for joining Freemasonry, my reason for visiting several NGOs, and looking for some opportunities to help out the needy. I was asked to figure out my passion. Figuring out my attachment became one of the most daunting tasks for me. While we were online in the session, I even went out to say that I couldn't figure out my passion. I felt I had no desire left to do something which I could place close to my heart. Nothing excites me anymore. My routine life was pretty okay, and I was thoroughly enjoying it. I was told that I was in my comfort zone and that big dreams can never be realized while living in a comfort zone. I never knew I enjoyed living in my comfort zone.

### *What's a Comfort zone:*

*For a person, a comfort zone is more psychological than physical. It's a relaxed state where you are not going to be tested. People tend to avoid trying new things or accepting any challenges. They exclusively engage in known activities, which gives them a sense of "control" over their environment and a feeling of being safe, but what they miss are thrills and challenges in life. It is said to change can only take place out of your comfort zone.* **"A step outside your comfort zone is a step into your miracle zone."—Cristie B Gardner.**

As passion is linked to purpose, I was disconnected from my goal as I lacked clarity on my interest. So, the first step was to identify my belonging. I brainstormed with my coach many times. However, during one of the sessions where we were almost thirty in the group, my coach suggested a way to find my purpose, and I was told to explore and note down all the reasons that make me happy. She was sure that if I did this exercise sincerely, I would know what my passion is, and once there is clarity on the force, the purpose will be straightforward to establish as there is a deep connection between the two. I liked the idea and started exploring and writing down all the possible reasons that made me happy. I noted all my small and significant achievements and accomplishments that gave me a sense of pride. The list went on and on, and by the time I stopped getting any further inputs, I had nearly fifty-one reasons responsible for making me happy.

**"No alarm clock needed. My passion wakes me."**– Eric Thomas.

Now, the next step was to get rid of things that only made me happy for a short time;
eating some rare exotic food
wearing a new brand shirt
getting a gift
being recognised for some accomplishments
getting a promotion
going to a place of my choice
getting an upgrade on the aircraft
buying a new pair of shoes
changing house furniture
getting a new property
making money in stock trends and many other things.

However, I could not relate them to the purpose of my life. They could be small goals accomplished, but nothing close to giving me meaning in my life, which I could call my "purpose of life".

After struggling for a pretty long time, I found all these reasons could be categorised into two parts:
1. What do I get?
2. What did I give?

An initiative of Mental Resilience Mastery © 2022

When I connected the dots, I discovered that most of my reasons fell into category 1: So, what do I get?

Except for a few exceptions, everything I listed was from category 1. There were only a few instances where I helped people through charity, donations, or gifts and brought smiles and cheer to them. Those were the times when I felt happy in an absolute sense. It wasn't momentary. The experience of such incidents has a long-lasting memory.

I XXXealized that receiving is short-lived and brings happiness for a short time, but giving is long-lived and can make you feel good, great, and happy for a longer duration.

I can now relate to my joining of Freemasonry. That also connects with my thought of giving, as it's founded on the three tenets, namely brotherly love, truth, and relief. The relief is one of the main pillars on which the entire Freemasonry stands. Here I found myself in the august company of all those brothers (we call them brethren) who love to give their time and money to help the needy or people in distress.

The point is that I was always attracted to all those activities where I could give my time, effort, and money to bring a smile to the faces of others. I even found myself more willing to help people I found to have some or other challenge. This affinity was XXXealized after a very long time.

## THE OUTCOME

We are all looking for ways and means to ease our lives. This ease is something we seek in all aspects of life, not just one. If you find your purpose, you will find the whole road map to lead your energy further. It will become an effortless and fulfilling journey. Once you have clarity on your purpose, you will be more focused, confident, and full of awareness. You will not find anything complicated but challenging. You will be able to operate your life from the paradigm of abundance and at a high vibrational frequency with no limiting beliefs and thoughts but always with empowering beliefs. The best part is that you will start empowering others with a paradigm shift in your life. Discovering your passion and purpose will lead to your ultimate desire, i.e., your "Grail." Now your life will tick to the right, with purpose: with your new GPS.

**Prabhunath Pandey:**
**linktr.ee/prabhunathp**

An initiative of Mental Resilience Mastery © 2022

## ELEVATE TO YOUR BEST SELF

My purpose decides my journey in life. Know your WHY!!

Knock Knock!

Who's there?

It's me, the inner child Tushar! May I have a minute to talk to you?

**Me:** Yes, please come in. I have been waiting to talk to you for quite a long time as there are certain things in my life that I'm still unsure about and want to explore. I'm looking for someone who could guide me and get me on the right track to know the purpose of my existence, and after exploring various dimensions and people, I now realise there is no one better than or superior to you, my dear inner self, to count on. I trust you entirely without a doubt that you would get me to the place or destination for which my soul has been in existence in this body form.

**Inner self:**Thank you for having unwavering faith in me, and now it becomes my responsibility to take you on your life journey. By the way, I came to talk to you regarding the same, as I was wondering whether you are lost in the pursuit of achieving materialistic gains and are utterly devoid of giving thought about your purpose in life. I am here to know your purpose in life, whether you are just serving the energy for being the kind of person you want to be or the kind of person people like you to be. Are you working on your dreams, or are you working on other peoples' dreams? What purpose drives you in your life and gives you a reason to get up in the morning? Have you given a thought to the questions below:

Who am I?
Why am I here?

**Me:** Yes, I have been talking to myself and venturing into different areas of my life. Initially, I was unaware; since childhood, I have been living my life as most people are guided by parents, elders, teachers and friends because it is the way life is meant to be. My life has been a beautiful journey of varied, rich experiences that have made me the person I am today. I am the result of my experiences and references drawn from this world and my karmic memories. My purpose in life is to evolve to a higher dimension beyond this world, purifying my soul and energies and touching the lives of people and every living being around me who come into my contact. My mind, body spirit should exude the powers that spread happiness and bliss everywhere around. I have heard about occult science. I want to know my relationship with the cosmos. I want to know my existence and touch the state of nothingness where I behold everything and find nothing more left to be explored, felt, touched and dreamt of.

I want to experience everything seen and unseen, as rightly put by John Keats in his "Ode on a Grecian urn" "Heard melodies are sweet, but those unheard are sweeter." The meaning is that the power of imagination is more significant than reality. I want to have a profound experience of everything preeminent and inconspicuous. My purpose is to be a vibrant enriching piece of life. If I wanted to define myself, I would like to be best described in the words of William Faulkner, "I always dream and shoot higher than I know I can do. I do not bother to be better than my contemporaries or predecessors. I always try to be better than myself every single day."

My purpose in life has not emerged in one night as Rome was not built in a day.

Similarly, my sense of life has taken years to build up. Since childhood, I have been raised in a spiritually enlightened set-up where positivity and divinity prevailed. I have grown up learning and imbibing these virtues consciously and subconsciously in myself, and these are the fundamental principles of life every child should be taught in their initial years. Seeing beyond the seen, feeling beyond the felt, and experiencing beyond the physical parameter has been my chase and desire. I choose to share things metaphysical because that is the ultimate truth. Not many get to know and read about it, forget about experiencing the same. I have to transcend the physical to reach the metaphysical and subsequently look at the world with a new perspective and vision.

**Inner self:** Are you aware of how to reach your ultimate goal?

**Me:** Once you are definite about your way in life, "HOW" becomes easy to find. I am drawing inspiration from various aspects, people, books, and experiences of myself and other people to reach my ultimate purpose. My recent learnings have been quite influential in breaking a few myths I have carried inside me for no joy. David Nair, my mentor, has taught me the power of "Faith, Commitment and Discipline", and I am profoundly taking the help of these guiding forces to reach my Everest. Disciplining my daily rituals, being in the association of mastermind people, and reading and listening to powerful content that has worked magic in the life of my predecessor, who had the same aspirations as me, will be my resources to anchor on.

Everything comes to us in the right moment and setting. However, we should strive hard to keep taking action and stay consistent in our efforts. Joyce Meyer rightly puts it forward, "Patience is not simply the ability to wait; it is how we behave while we are waiting". As I try to behave sanely while I stay patient to achieve everything that I have dreamt of to take myself one level up to attain my actual level of existence. I believe that if you have the right mentors, the best intent and the ability to work on specific disciplines in your life, nothing can deter you from achieving what you aspire to.

**Inner self:** What is the outcome of your why?

**Me:** My "WHY" will undoubtedly impact my life and the people around me concerning every minute cell and item surrounding my inner and outer being. The people in control and are in charge of their life can be role models for others. As a famous quote says, "A leader is one who knows the way, goes the way and shows the way."

So, if I want to show people the road to success and fulfilment of their dreams and aspirations, I have to walk the same road barefoot to get every harrowing experience to be able to share my story with them. My learnings and challenges will also pave the way for them and prepare them to walk the path. I will be a role model only if I have the same experience. I need to walk the talk and then talk tall to make a massive impact. I want to hold the hand of every single soul who wants to go on a journey of self-exploration. There is no gain without pain. So those who are ready to feel the pain, get out of their comfort zone and challenge their limiting belief is most welcome to come on this beautiful journey called "LIFE".

Remember:
**"When it rains, look for rainbows."**
Or, to put it in other words,
"It has to rain for there to be a rainbow".

I pen down with firm faith in the supreme power that is ruling the world, which
An initiative of Mental Resilience Mastery © 2022

controls the alignment of planets and related objects, that takes care of the existence of every atom and cell of this universe.

"Your word is a lamp to my feet and a light to my path."
(Psalms 119:105)

**Inner self:** I am so glad you are on this journey of self-exploration and trust me, I will always be your support which will always help you decide between two choices in your life that will shape your purpose. Good Luck!!

An initiative of Mental Resilience Mastery © 2022

**Tushar Bhargava:**
https://linktr.ee/tushar_2022

## UNDERSTANDING MY WHY- MY IKIGAI

**Your calling isn't something that somebody can tell you about. It's what you feel, the thing that gives you juice. You know it inside yourself."**
**-OPRAH WINFREY**

What is your purpose? Why am I here? I believe we are born for a purpose bigger than ourselves. I have got some insights that I am sharing with you.

My purpose is to inspire, inform and ignite the spark of self-love, to transform the lives of 1000 men and women who are facing emotional challenges and are burdened by their emotional baggage of past blunders, wrong choices, shame, and guilt. By raising their self-esteem, they can lead productive, creative, and fulfilling personal and professional lives. By stopping their inner chatter, they can express their feelings and find their voice to be happy and live authentically.

My vision is of a community of emotionally resilient men and women living in emotional freedom, with a thriving mindset and creating harmony and balance in their lives by aligning their life goals with their values. My personal

An initiative of Mental Resilience Mastery © 2022

experience in my 20s may have influenced my decision.

I am Vaijayanti Bose; Teacher turned Coach and Speaker, now the Founder of my Mastermind for Emotional Expression, EXPRESS, AND THRIVE. An author, blogger, and podcaster, I am a senior Rotarian leader in District 3291 and Past President of my Club, Rotary Club of Calcutta Samaritans. Of late, I have joined Toastmasters International to hone my public speaking skills and communicate my vision more effectively to my audience.

Ever since I was old enough to think about my future profession, the only choice open to me was a teacher's 'noble' profession. I stumbled onto teaching without a preconceived plan when the Principal of the Ramakrishna Mission School, Along with Arunachal Pradesh, invited me to join his institution to teach English to the first generation of tribal learners. I enjoyed my stint teaching there, as their young minds were like a clean slate, ready to absorb whatever they were taught. My father was Deputy Commissioner, Along, and I was back home after graduation, mulling over my next step. On returning to Kolkata, I enrolled in a B. Ed course in my alma mater, Loreto College, preparing for a teaching career. I did make one last effort to do something pathbreaking in those days. Egged on by my aunt, who was my role model, I applied for an advertised position at Oberoi Grand Hotel. My interview went off so well that I was offered the appointment of Assistant Housekeeper, subject to the training they would conduct to prepare me for my new role. I returned to my grandfather's place, where I was staying then, with my head floating on cloud nine. I had a vision of being trained in Switzerland, but my hopes were dashed to the ground as soon as I told my grandfather about the irresistible offer.

Assuming his Victorian persona, he boomed out in his authoritative voice, "No granddaughter of mine is going to be a glorified ayah, cleaning up people's mess," that put pause to my technicolour dreams of joining the Hotel Industry, travelling the world and meeting new people. I was tongue-tied and dumbfounded and caved in without a single word, as he was then my guardian in Calcutta. So, I reconciled myself to my dismal future as a school teacher. But I was soon to be engulfed by the love of my students and would find my passion and purpose in teaching.

My teaching career spanned four satisfying decades, teaching History and

English to girls in the middle and senior classes of well-known institutions in my city and preparing them for debates and public speaking competitions. The last 36 years were spent in the Tollygunge unit of the Ashok Hall Group of Schools. As Faculty Coordinator, I helped them to develop their creative and leadership skills through active participation in the activities of the school chapter of SPICMACAY and the projects of Bichitra Pathshala. These are NGOs working with educational institutions for the holistic development of youth. I enjoyed ten years post-retirement extension of service, but from 2019, I started looking around for a possible career path for my second innings, as I was not ready to hang up my boots.

I came across Peak Performance Coach Arfeen Khan's Coach Training Program and felt it was the answer to all my questions. By the end of the year, I had completed my three months of training and got duly certified as a Mindset Coach for his ICF-accredited Incredible You Program. Thus, I began my journey as a coach but was I looking for something else?

I found my answer when attending the Coach to Fortune Mega Event at Sahara

Star, Mumbai, in March 2020. I saw the power of Arfeen as a Coach and Speaker at very close quarters. Public Speaking has been my dream since I was placed first in an Extempore Speech Contest in school, and I found the pathway to becoming one in Arfeen's program for Speakers. At that time, this Speak to Fortune program was very different, wherein we had to create our programs. Still, the outbreak of the Corona Pandemic changed everything, as Arfeen decided to go online and make a new Mastermind Edition, whereby we would run our Masterminds depending on the Niche and Sub-niche we selected for ourselves. This gift from our Mentor far exceeded our expectations- by giving us a ready-to-use customized program and weekly training on marketing our Masterminds by his Super Coaches, he set us on the road to launch our own business.

I have impacted more than 4000 lives of teenage children during my teaching years. I had counselled them through the turbulent years of high school frustration and failures and fashioned them into strong women of character who could face the world on their terms, following their passion. Now, I want to expand that experiential learning beyond the classroom to inform, educate and transform the mindset of those women who were conditioned from their childhood to think small and muzzle their authentic voices. I wanted the

members of my Club take ownership of their voice, ascend from victimhood to become the hero of their Life Story, and thrive in abundance.

Initially, I had decided to focus on women from thirty to sixty years of age, who had been conditioned from childhood not to assert themselves and repress their emotions, to be ladylike. Still, when I started running my mastermind on a virtual platform, I discovered that some men also had emotional roadblocks, were stuck in their past stories and were looking for the path to emotional freedom. So, I ran two masterminds on an experimental basis, one for both men and women, and the members experienced magical breakthroughs. This is how I found my tagline. "Own your Voice for a Magical Life."

A year back, to help women acquire strong self-worth to become unstoppable, I wrote a book, PIVOT IN CONFIDENCE Live Carefree. Its central theme is the importance of Change. Change is vital for growth- change in mindset, physical health, or career if we want to enhance our self-image and personal and professional relationships. The book illustrates this idea through tools and strategies to acquire empowering mental codes of behaviour and real-life narratives of confident, booming, and happy women in my close circle, who overcame complex challenges, to emerge triumphant in their professional domains.

Coming to my Mastermind, EXPRESS AND THRIVE- Own your Voice for a Magical Life…. It has five specific Outcomes:

❖STEP UP- Stepping up from living in fear and low self-worth.

❖LET GO- Letting go of your deepest, toxic feelings in a supportive and non-judgmental space.

❖GET BETTER- Healed from within by sharing your past story and understanding how it made you a better person.

❖MOVE AHEAD- Moving forward with pride and conviction in your worth.

❖LEVEL UP- Expanding your passion into a purposeful business to enjoy financial independence.

My Masterminds are for people keen to become a better version of themselves and are willing to invest in their continual growth. Although each mastermind will be a journey of three months, the Facebook group will continue as a space for exchanges and collaboration among its members. I intend the virtual platform to grow into a powerful channel of mutual growth by sharing the members' expertise and domain knowledge with each other.

It is in giving that we receive and in seeking that we find.
"ONLY BY GIVING ARE YOU ABLE TO RECEIVE MORE THAN YOU ALREADY HAVE." JIM ROHN

**Vaijayanti Bose :**
https://linktr.ee/vijii.bose.

## INFLUENCERS RECOMONDATION

"I know people who frequently change gurus in their search for the Holy Grail. To stop searching for it, you must be aware of this fact.

An initiative of Mental Resilience Mastery © 2022

This book examines thirty global influencers' pursuit of life's meaning. In each chapter, the reader is taken on a journey through the life of a different character. The dunes appeared intimidating before they saw the glimmering hope of their life's purpose. Strongness, passion, and clarity are just a few subthemes that the reader can explore.

According to a book, you can reach your goal no matter how high the mountain is. Humans have a strong will to live. Follow your heart, and you'll discover your life's purpose."

-Sandeep Chalke
Practicing professional with over 20 years of experience of Governance, Risk Management and Compliance
www.isomantra.com

"Grail"-Tick Your Life Right, With Purpose, is a unique project which is a compilation of the views of 30 different authors.

A life without a purpose is a listless journey where a human being is reduced to a dried autumn leaf, spinelessly blowing in the wind. Purpose in life drives us to achieve our goals and helps us find happiness through achievements. This project is extremely significant in today's day where our world is slowly but certainly evolving from a brick-and-mortar world, to a virtual one.

This is a commendable project as it is an anthology of a multi-dimensional approach consisting of diverse views and experiences. Collective wisdom is something that one can always rely on, as the advice comes based on various experiences, mainly when these experiences come from people who have walked the talk.

I wish David Nair, all the success that this charitable project so richly deserves and may the valuable views of the various authors weaved into this book, reach as many people as possible so that their lives may be transformed into happier ones, turning them into achievers with a purpose and a life worth living.

-Ralph de Sousa
Group Chairman, de Souza group
President Goa Chamber of Commerce

# CLARITY

## DARE TO DREAM

**"A good plan, violently executed now is better than a perfect plan tomorrow."**
**George Patton**

Many of us have dreams and passions, and we always strive to turn them into reality, but a lack of clarity, guidance and proper strategic road maps prevent us from achieving them. Sometimes the fear of failures, past bitter experiences, criticism and intimidating business challenges make us so scared that even we forget our long-cherished dreams and passions. My purpose is to help people to turn their ideas and passions into genuine products and services without making costly mistakes. Never let them settle for less. Help them explore their hidden and latent talents. Every bud deserves to blossom and stun the world with its exceptional beauty and fragrance.

I am Bashir Haroon, a business and performance coach, author, speaker, and trainer. I started my career as an entrepreneur in the garment export sector at a very early age. Still, the 2009 recession had given me a different opportunity to improve my people management skills and help them recognize their real potential and dormant talents. Working as an HR professional with Aramco associate company has allowed me to meet and listen to the thousands of skills forced to work for lesser positions due to different circumstances. I put myself in their shoes and found myself very close to them to know and analyze the real situations that lead people to settle for less than they deserve. I started trying to help them reach their potential and recognize their natural talents. I help many to realize never to sell themselves short and strive to become more significant than the moments. Many of them started believing that situations could not decide their destiny. They are more effective than the moment, and only their decision and powerful choices can determine their future. In any case, they are capable enough to raise the bar to become their best version. My support and eagerness started yielding excellent results. This has given me the courage to go deeper and start doing this on a more extensive scale. The impact would be more significant, and the result would be remarkable.

Covid-19 has given me another opportunity to share my ideas in a proper shape and business model by doing it more professionally. I enrolled in a life coaching program and was associated as a certified life coach with Arfeen Khan and his Incredible You Coaching Program, which is ICF-approved.

My purpose is my North Star. I also come from the same background, and I lacked direction and guidance at any point in my career. This had not only cost me financial loss but forced me to settle for less on many occasions and deprived me of achieving what could I deserve. Sometimes even I realize that dreaming big is also daunting. If somebody thinks that dreaming big and having great ideas and passions are scary, it is a serious issue and should be dealt with proper care and diligence.

I have made costly mistakes due to a lack of clear guidance and a proper road map. Support someone who will at least understand and admit that the idea is legit and has potential. At least, if not unable to comprehend, never discourage someone. Because after discouragement, the pain and trauma become severe and sometimes devastating. I do not want others to ever go into that zone. Not pursuing your dreams and not executing your valuable ideas stop you from flourishing personally and make precious ideas not even be introduced to the world and shed light on them, which might contribute to the progression of humanity and may resolve some real challenges that bother many of us. Who knows, once the idea takes shape, it could stun the world and provide a new direction to the world. It could create magic and could change history. Ideas without execution are nothing, but after performance could make a miracle and bring the revolution.

After becoming a certified Coach, I clarified my vision more and started working on my prototype with some of my close friends and aspirational clients. The result is far more excellent than expected. It has boosted my confidence, and my energy level is hugely beefed up. I am in the process of making this a great business and training model where I could help individuals and business to carve their ideas and passions and turn them into Minimal Viable Products with proper guidance and support at an affordable price.

The ideas and execution are both critical; without evaluating the arguments and understanding clearly, we would not be able to bring some real value. A vision without execution is merely a concept. Having great ideas and passion and executing them right is vital. It creates real magic. Performance not only helps to nurture and give the proper shape to the concept, but it tests the real potential and viability. It makes it outshine. It makes the success real. This daunting and intimidating process deters many from even thinking about the execution part.

Here comes my fundamental role, I help individuals and businesses:
· How to recognise the viability of the idea.
· How to know the challenges of executing the idea.
· How to validate your ideas, identify your market, and get ahead of your competitors.
· How to Craft monetisation Strategy and Solid Financial Model of Your Business. · How to understand the root of the problem you aim to solve and craft your USP Unique Selling Point/ Proposition.
· Prototyping and iterating
· Building a Great Team
· Achieving remarkable growth in your personal and professional life.

By providing these foundations and step-by-step guidance and support and iterating the tested models at a larger scale. I want to create an atmosphere where people cannot feel afraid to validate, implement, and execute their ideas for fear of failure or lack of guidance and support. Test to become the best. Magic is **"Ideas are yesterday, execution is today and excellence will see you into tomorrow."**

**-Julian Hall**

**Bashir Haroon:**
**https://linktr.ee/Bashirharoon**
**Jeddah KSA**

An initiative of Mental Resilience Mastery © 2022

## HIGHEST VIBRATION WINS: REGAIN

## BELIEF | RE-CONNECT | RE-ENERGISE

*I have a dream. That one day, all of God's children will be able to join hands and sing. Free at last! Free at last! Thank God Almighty, we are free at last!*
-Martin Luther King Jr, at the Lincoln Memorial, Washington D.C.

A girl, who has always dreamt big, and thought everything is possible, somehow, limitations, specific standards, and expectations were fed into her mind, including one who scores excellent marks in class will do great in life. She was made to believe that she was a good girl. But she was meant to taste both success and failures!

Hello, I am Amanpreet Kaur, daughter of my proud parents, elder sister of two supportive & lovable siblings, and blessed with two beautiful children and a fantastic husband. I have always believed I can fill the lives I touch with rhythm and music through limitless divine intelligence, the source.

I am the Mental Toughness & Happiness Coach, Gut Health Mentor, Collagen consultant, and morning routine specialist.

An initiative of Mental Resilience Mastery © 2022

Founder of 'mywellbeing365days',
'extreme. energyclubbyaman', 'Believe in You, Lady' and an author.

*"A man cannot be comfortable without his approval."*
-Mark Twain

1. "You haven't learned anything. You do not know how to manage your home, family, and work. You are the most unorganized person. Poor management.
I have been hearing this for 11 years.
Feeling: Experienced Discomfort. Unhappiness (Victim State)

2. "You have done a tremendous job. You have managed everything well, super." It is the first time I'm hearing this in years.
Feeling: Experienced peace (State of awareness)

The question I asked myself was: Am I seeking validation or approval? Why is an appreciation not making me happy, though? I have secretly wished for it for years!

The above two statements have come from the same person in different situations. One word is common in these: manage-me-n (o)t. And it comes from managing myself (manage me). While working with corporate, I was in the management team, dealt with 1000s of people, and promoted a great work culture that inspired and enabled building character with harmony and joy, resulting in a great outcome.

An initiative of Mental Resilience Mastery © 2022

In the past, I managed things, managed people at home and the office, and tried to fix them. Consequently, I failed. I forgot to address and love myself because I was off purpose and needed to work on myself.

*"The time will arrive when you start to feel beautiful, despite all the criticism and negative forces and energies that surround you on a physical plane, and at that time, you will start to act beautifully on autopilot mode in congruence with your purpose."*
-Amanpreet Kaur

The Almighty has already put the best machinery in each being in this universe originally. And we imagine that we are not good enough. What we have to recover is our original unity. That is oneness inside out. I failed to love and trust myself and denied that infinite wisdom favours my ego. Very well put by Dr Wayne Dyer:

*"When you love and trust yourself, you love and trust the wisdom that created you."*

**Victim mentality:** Why did I fail to experience joy and happiness within me and always feel upset? Though I did my best to make people happy around me, most of my time I spent in a low energetic state of shame, regret/guilt, complaint, etc. People's comments bothered me so much since childhood, and I got hurt. Why did I always feel a lack of focus and self-esteem? Why did I never accept myself the way I was created?

People around me doubted my abilities, so I also started to lose faith in myself because I believed in what they said about me! I felt I had no worth.

**Have you ever experienced this kind of situation in your life when you started to doubt yourself for anything you do?**

So, my ego dominated me. The good news is that even during the low state, I was driven by the need to understand myself (stand up for myself – seemed secondary this time), to do something for people in the context of love and joy, to give, to raise my energy levels and to connect with the source that created me. At the same time, my victim outlook stopped me from jumping out of my comfort zone. I was disconnected from my roots.

**Awareness:**

*"When she realized her self-worth, the game changed. The perspective towards herself and others took 360 degrees turn. And she began to find joy and unconditional love in herself and everyone. She understood the laws of Abundance and Prosperity: You ask with sanctified intention, and it will be given. "*

-Amanpreet

Primarily, the spiritual awareness and self-introspection helped me dive deep within myself, take a RAHAO (pause) & be mindful of the thoughts and stories my monkey mind narrated. I got to know how my energy was impacting the people around me. Also, the views of building mental resilience in me started to take shape.

**An Eye-Opener Fact:**According to Dr Hawkin's 29-year study and research, "One individual who lives and vibrates to the energy of optimism and a willingness to be non-judgmental of others will counterbalance the negativity of 90,000 individuals who calibrate at the lower weakening levels." How powerful is that!

I never knew I have so much power within. **So, you have, my dear!**

High-energy people counterbalance the energy of low-energy people. One person connected to intention can enormously impact many people in lower energy patterns. The higher up the scale you move toward actually being the light of enlightenment and knowing God's consciousness, the more negatively vibrating energies you can counterbalance. Now discovering ways of improving human consciousness and raising ourselves to the place where we match up with the same point of intention from which we were. By boosting your frequency of vibration slightly to a position where you regularly practice kindness, love, and receptivity, and where you see the beauty and the endless potential of good in others as well as yourself, you counterbalance 90,000 people somewhere on this planet who are living the low-energy levels of shame, anger, hatred, guilt, despair, and depression. Isn't it amazing?

The irony is that I thought negative energies/people around me surrounded me, and they did not understand me; I forgot to cater to the energy I was embodying! I didn't listen to my inner voice, my true self.

*"No mind can fully know the true self or internal light, but the true self and internal light know whatever mind does."*

-Rahao School of Life.

**Experience with my daughter:** The agony, hurt, and regret I was carrying in my head resulted in bodily pains. One 'dark' night, I was profoundly crying within and couldn't stop my tears (successfully hidden from her) while lying on the bed with my 7.5-year-old daughter. She couldn't sleep and conveyed," Mumma, I feel headache on my left part of head and stomach ache on the right side." I was taken aback because I could sense the pains in the same areas of my body and hadn't shared them with her. It was an alarm for me as it had happened once before. It was the time to step up and heal myself, as I could see how my vibration was transferred to her, affecting her physically.

An initiative of Mental Resilience Mastery © 2022

With the help of my Shabad Guru and my Coaches, I discovered that those who feel purposeful possess the highest humanitarian qualities on this planet. Many of the problems in my life resulted because I was disconnected from intention and purpose and hence was unaware of my true identity.

**Surrender:**I surrendered to the universe.

It was high time for me to reconnect with my intention to live my life on purpose, including building and rejuvenating holy relationships that already existed in my life. I realized that everyone in this universe is connected to the invisible force called intention and that everything is sourced from this energy, this limitless divine intelligence. I was awestruck by the very fact of my existence. And begin to get clarity on purpose. What had been happening in our lives, in my life, was nothing accidental. My journey to embracing one and all commenced (be it my children, my husband, my parents, my siblings, relatives, and unknown people around.)

Our Spiritual Master Guru Gobind Singh quoted,"***TREAT ALL HUMAN RACE AS ONE.***"(manas ki jaat sabhai ekai pehchanbo). Now I understood what HE meant.

**Discovery:** Your purpose is not about what you do but about how you feel.

An initiative of Mental Resilience Mastery © 2022

Feeling purposeful activates your power of intention to create anything. You intend to live your life on purpose.

Initially, I was getting questions about my existence. What am I doing with my life? Am I supposed to be a housewife or a working professional? Am I fulfilling my true purpose? What do I love to do? Am I dwelling in love while I do my daily chores? When you are awake enough to question your purpose, ask your intuition, and how to connect to it, you are being prodded by the power of intention. If you are questioning, it's a clear symbol that your thoughts are nudging you to reconnect to the field of intention. You will find ways to sit with yourself daily and meditate to awaken your intuition.

When you are in the service of others or extend kindness beyond your boundaries, you will feel connected to your source. You will feel happy and content knowing that you are doing the right thing. The very existence of human beings is BE-ING, not DO-ING.

When I take a moment to cheer people around me when I make children laugh who feel ignored if I extend my assistance to someone in need while travelling or anywhere; when I cook for the family; when I coach people who ask for help, etc. I feel connected: which is aligned with my purpose. I feel blissful and purposeful when I act to serve others instead of inflating my ego. Being on purpose may not necessarily reap monetary benefits; it may be a by-product, but what you become during your journey makes all the difference. We have to let go of the ego that tries to separate us from Ultimate Truth and the originating divine source, divine intelligence. Only then, your thoughts about your purpose would reconnect with your inner being.

**My purpose in life is**

*"To Live in and work in a prosperous environment that encourages productivity and happiness and promotes growth so that I can improve the service I render to my family, my community, and the world at large".*

I worked on reconnecting with my intention through our infinite divine source and realigning with my purpose first. Yes, I have taken a Leap of faith and already started working towards the impact I can have on our civilization/humanity, being on higher runs on the ladder to intention. As I established good relationships with myself, other relationships in my life have improved, and I have become respectful and loving. My personal and professional life is balanced. And I feel like I am living in heaven. It is rightly said, "Be the change you want to see in thc world".

An initiative of Mental Resilience Mastery © 2022

Give love to receive it; give happiness to receive it. Whatever you want to get, first provide that through your service or with your presence by maintaining your own high energy vibrational levels (& create a high energy field around), then observe the difference you have made in others' lives and made them feel great in one way or another. Let's strive for excellence instead of perfection.**Your source has completed your validation process before sending you on this planet. Do you still need validation/ approval from others? Reminder**: If you still feel so, reconnect with your source, your inner being, your true self, and your pure intention. You will get all the answers.

"Believe in you" because you are a piece of God, HIS unique, beautiful creation, and you are on purpose. You are abundant. Believe that prosperity flows through you. Ask yourself, "**Would you doubt HIS creation, doubt 'yourself'?" Would you not believe in yourself?** Are you committed to yourself?

Let your presence allows others to feel unified. Let's vibrate to the higher levels of consciousness because the Highest Vibration Wins.

Experience Life, Well Lit.

**Amanpreet Kaur:**
https://linktr.ee/coachamanpreet

An initiative of Mental Resilience Mastery © 2022

## LIFE ITSELF REVEALS ITS PURPOSE -

## IT'S PASSION

Several years back, it might be around 2016, and I recall sitting on my couch and realizing that no desires were left in me: neither worldly nor spiritual desires. There is no impetus to act. There is nothing to chase.

So, I asked the all-knowing Divine Power: "Please tell me why am I still on this planet? This magic carpet ride of life, this beautiful gift, has brought me to a point of total fulfilment and contentment. I am happy just being. I feel complete. Nothing shakes me, and nothing pulls me. I am not attracted to anything nor am I opposed to anything. It is like Ansuya does not exist. Then what is the purpose for this life still here on this planet? Even the desire to chase to serve others is no more and even the ultimate desire for achieving enlightenment has dropped. Yet I am happy. If I am still here, then I guess YOU have a purpose for my life. Then so be it. You can use my life to fulfil your Divine will or not use my life I am ok with either."

When you converse with the Universe from a deep, authentic space, the supreme power always responds sooner or later. In

2021 the Universe showed me the ultimate purpose of my life. Here is my story of how I was led to this purpose.

I was born in 1960 in Durban, South Africa, to immigrant parents from India. For my first 11 years, we lived in a joint extended family system. We were 16 children altogether in one apartment. It was a hard life for my parents, doing their best to keep us fed, clothed, and educated in apartheid, South Africa. For us children, it was much fun to have so many playmates; I recall having loads of playtime and being filled with Joy.

Hence the **first seed** for my life purpose was planted.

Discover and live your joy.

My parents did not get on too well, but they loved us children. My mother struggled as she could not live the life she wanted to. A patriarchal society would not support her studying English and being a Gujarati school teacher. She attempted but could not claim her power to stand up to societal pressure. An Indian woman cannot go out there. It pained me to see my unconditionally loving mother struggle.

The **second seed** of my current life purpose was planted.

We need to claim our power and live our dreams.

After completing my schooling, I enrolled for Engineering Degree. It was the freedom struggle years of the late 1970s. Staying focused was a challenge. Hence, I had a few successful and a few unsuccessful years of Engineering studies. The failure was challenging, but later it proved to be the best thing. It was the trigger to move to Johannesburg, at 23, in search of work.

The **third seed** was planted.

Failure is not what it seems; it is the beginning of new possibilities.

I got lost in the big city of Johannesburg. I went through lots of tough times and gained lots of life experience. At age 26, I met my spouse. He brought stability into my life. I worked and studied part-time to complete my Computer Science and Information Systems honours degree. I worked in substantial international corporations, enjoyed my work and earned well. I travelled globally for work and had excellent holidays with my friends and spouse. Despite all this, I still experienced the ups and downs of worldly life. My mind tended towards stress, anxiety, frustration, anger, doubt, etc. I observed that my spouse would expect positive effects while I was doubtful and expected adverse effects. He was much more accepting of situations, whereas I continuously wanted situations to be a certain way. Whenever there was a challenge, my mind would go to the route cause to look for a solution while his mind would respond directly to the challenge.

Observing these contrasting mindsets and their effects planted the **fourth seed**.

Our attitude impacts not only our life but also affects the lives of those in our space.

My spouse and I were interested in health, and we started our healthy lifestyle journey and continuously learnt and implemented it. We experienced the different impacts of foods on the body and mind. I stopped getting the flu; it was more apparent in my thinking, and my energy levels improved.

The **fifth seed** of my life purpose was planted.

A healthy lifestyle impacts the body and mind. I would never have guessed then that I would someday author a book on a Healthy Lifestyle.
So much was going well for me, so why did I feel like something was still missing? This gap drove me to embark on a

spiritual search at 27. I joined a yoga class, and eventually, at age 37, I met one of my spiritual teachers, Gurudev Sri Sri Ravi Shankar, founder of The Art of Living Organization (AOL). I attended every spiritual program offered by AOL several times. These were Yoga, breathing techniques, meditation, and silence retreats, among many others.

I began to grow in my wisdom of the Self, and my awareness continuously expanded. As the stresses and strains fell away, my sense of belongingness expanded. I lived more in the present moment. I noticed my world perception changing for the better. I started to become unshakable in my emotions. Anxiety and negative thoughts began to diminish.

I became more creative in my thinking.
Judgements dropped.
My relationships improved.
Sleep improved.
Energy increased.
My vibratory level increased.
My experience was deep and powerful, and I knew I had to share these learnings with others.

Hence, in 2004 I received my certification to teach Yoga. It gave me joy to watch my students get healthier and calmer. Over the following years, I qualified to teach the powerful Sudarshan Kriya Breathing technique, meditation, and the AOL Prison program. I am also certified in the ancient healing therapeutic arts of Marma and Rakkenho. I was still working in my corporate career. It was like holding two jobs, yet I was enjoying it. My time with AOL was like a magic carpet ride. It was filled with many experiences of profound revelations of the working of an unseen power beyond this gross world and a deeper understanding of this vile world.

The **sixth seed** was planted.

Connection to the Self makes life magical, and sharing increases joy.
At age 45, my spouse and I decided to separate after 20 years together. Over the years, my mother, father, sister and brother all passed on. Fortunately, my spiritual wisdom kept me in a good and robust space. Thanks to my spiritual learnings, I had no bitterness, sadness, or anger in my heart.
The Universe started unfolding the answer to my question in 2016. If there are no desires left and yet I am happy, what is there to do? Here is where it all changed.

In 2021 I lost my life savings to someone I trusted dearly. The Universe cleverly gave me a reason to act again. My life experience kept my mind in a good space.

**The seeds had been planted.**

If I must earn again, it will have to be through a passion for empowering people. Within a few days, by chance, I came across Arfeen Khan's Incredible You Coach Training program. I enrolled, and a whole new world opened. It has been an eye-opening journey. The program ignited that spark for Living (a mission and a passion) and beautifully complimented my residing in Being (happy and content). The best of both the seen and the unseen world.

My mission and purpose were born.
The seeds had blossomed.
I will coach to transform 10 000 beautiful souls to live their Best Lives Ever.
To get them unstuck in areas of relationships, career, and health. They will gain clarity, gain vitality, uncover their power, claim back their dreams, uncover their passions and their talents, rejoice in their full potential, turn failures into new possibilities, connect to the Self and share their gifts to make a difference in the world. Their outcome will be; that when

they reach the last days of their lives and look back; they will say, "That is the life I wanted to live. It was the Best Life ever".

Ansuya Khoosal is a certified health and life transformation coach. She is an author, a healing therapist, and a teacher of Yoga, breathwork and meditation. She uses her life experience and Arfeen Khan's ICF-certified coaching program to coach her client's gain clarity and transformation in the areas of Self, relationships, career, and health. Her clients gain empowered mindsets and live their Best Life ever. She loves spending time in nature, reading,

learning about the world, and connecting to people.
**You can contact Ansuya at https://linktr.ee/ansuyakhoosal.**

## HAPPINESS IS A CHOICE

I am Dr Fauzia Shamshad. I have done my PhD in Psychology from Aligarh Muslim University, Aligarh. In my research, I have studied the effect of meditation and cognitive intervention and a combination of both (meditation and cognitive intervention) on a person high in Neuroticism. Neuroticism is a personality trait that tends to cause negative emotions. The research was conducted on four groups of people; the first group learned meditation to deal with negative emotions. The second group learned cognitive intervention only. The third group learned meditation and cognitive intervention to deal with negative sentiments. The fourth group did not know anything but was observed for three months, like the other three groups.

The result was astonishing as all the people in the three groups improved tremendously in different areas of their lives. They all reported that after participating, their life had improved a lot. Their perspective toward the problem has changed. They found themselves happier now.

My research has given me evidence that when a person takes a responsibility to change their mindset can result in a happier and more fulfilled life.

My confidence became my belief during my practice days when I worked with a physician at Bansal Hospital, Ghaziabad. She was a gold medallist in medicine and heart specialist. Working with her, I saw how people had changed their life from being miserable to more fulfilling and happier. They changed their belief system in dealing with negative emotions and completely eliminated their heart problems. It gives me immense pleasure to prove that when people's relationship issues get resolved, they learn better ways to deal with life's challenges. Their physical health was also improved.

Through these stories, I observed that people negatively interpret issues in their relationship with their spouse, children, or themselves. They can enjoy their life by changing these emotions into positive ones. This observation gave me confidence, and I have treated patients with Anxiety, OCD, and Depression successfully.

The time of the pandemic was fruitful for me; I utilized that time for my learning and growth. I learned NLP, Hypnotherapy, and also a course on Life Coach. By Comprehending all my knowledge and experience, I am on a mission to impact the lives of 1 million people to make their lives happier.

**My Purpose**
My purpose is to make people realize that the happiest person is the one who has a healthy and supportive relationship with themself and the other people around them. The relationship with others is the reflection of the relationship one has with themselves. Now I am on the mission to inspire, educate and help people have loving or fulfilling relationships with themselves and others.

An initiative of Mental Resilience Mastery © 2022

Happiness is the ultimate goal of any individual on this earth. No matter what worldly or personal goal one has. It is always the feeling of happiness attached to a particular aim when achieved.

When we were kids, we used to play with friends, and we enjoyed and experienced happiness. Then playing with them, we got some toys, and then there was an increment in our level of satisfaction. From then, we started associating our "happiness" with the toy. If I could have this toy, I would be happy. We started thinking "happiness means to have"
As we started going to school, whenever we got good marks or performed some tasks and achieved some awards, we started thinking that "happiness means to achieve."

When a person becomes mature and starts taking responsibility for their lives and doing things for others, they realize the happiness/joy of giving and start thinking that "happiness means to give."

After connecting the dots of my life. Standing where I am today, the literature I have gone through, the people I have consoled, and the lesson I learned has taught me that "happiness means to be
_____."

One doesn't have to have something to achieve something or give something to be happy. Happiness means to be .........
Happiness means to be...... there for someone.
Happiness means to be ....... with someone.

It is not the toy or target, or gift that brings happiness. The company of friends or upscaling ourselves or someone's presence brings us joy, but we have misinterpreted happiness and created a vacuum.

With the constant comparison of ourselves with others and society. We have forgotten our true nature, our likes, and our dislikes. The influence of social media has developed a mob mentality in people, and they have started accumulating worldly wealth at the cost of their health and relationship. Later in life, they achieve their target but still have a vacuum in themselves. And they cannot find happiness as they don't have health or people to celebrate their achievements.

People who live intending to return also create a vacuum in their lives. According to the law of nature, we do not get returns from the person we give. The Universe has its way of returning the things we shared, and one must learn to surrender to the law of the Universe. Sometimes people who are givers create misery for themselves by giving too much. They drain themselves and get disheartened, which also affects one's health.

My purpose is to help people realize what actually, happiness is. And how they can be true to themselves, which in return will make them emotionally and mentally strong. That they can face the challenges of life and still be happy.
Life becomes difficult when one starts giving importance to worldly things in place of humans. We think things provide happiness, but in reality, if we don't have anyone to share our joy with, we feel a vacuum inside ourselves. We cannot experience true love, peace, or happiness by going against the law of nature. We feel powerful by being independent, but nature has made us interdependent. When we realize the power of interdependence, we feel empowered.

I will feel blessed if I can help people to make their life happier and empowered.

**Dr. Fauzia Shamshad:**
https://linktr.ee/dr_fauzia

An initiative of Mental Resilience Mastery © 2022

## EMBRACE YOUR POWER

My purpose in life is to reach out to millions of women and youngsters to reinvent their passion and rediscover their true dream mission.

In life, we as women are always tutored from childhood that we must take care of our household chores, and we are the primary caregivers in our family. Our dreams and our goals are secondary, and it takes backstage. Now times have changed, but the responsibility remains the same. Unless we women find a supportive spouse and a family that encourages us to move ahead with our dream.

As women, our duty is our family's smooth functioning and well-being. With the arrival of a child in a family, we give ourselves ultimately to nurture the child, his education, and his future. Subsequently, attending to the ailing in-laws or their medical needs, extending a helping hand to the other members of the family, dealing with the demands of our husbands at times and bearing the tantrums of all. In all these situations, we are the central pillar of the family, and everything revolves around us. Our dreams, desires, goals, and mission take a secondary position.

You are never too old to follow your passion and reinvent yourself. Age is just a number that tells us we still have many things to accomplish. We should not put our attachment aside but, daily, reinvent ourselves towards achieving it. There comes the point when you have to take that leap of faith and get started. For me, this meant taking life/relationship coaching as my passion. Taking this decision has not been an easy task. I faced many hurdles like financial issues, no support from my spouse, household responsibilities and low self-esteem. Fortunately, this did not stop me from moving ahead with my dreams.

Recently, our youth are caught up in the rat race of competing with each other, be it in getting good scores in their examination, fulfilling their parent's dream, peer pressure, and not the least to stand out in society. In this mad race, youngsters have forgotten their true self and their true calling. They often get misled, mentally and physically abused, and fall prey to bad company.

Youth nowadays are more confused and depressed than youth 50 to 60 years back. I think it's because of the advent of the internet and social media. Social media exposes young minds to many things that affect them positively and negatively. Young people, these days get easily depressed at the slightest things, for example, seeing someone live a good life on Facebook, probably by taking pictures that depict such ideas, pictures of them travelling, clubbing, driving fancy cars etc. so the one who is missing all the fun, tend to be jealous and think their life sucks. The glitter and charm of city life lure young minds of small towns and villages toward the metropolitan city. The old saying goes, "the grass is always greener on the other side".

Hello everyone, I take pleasure in introducing myself. My name is Rosy Regina Barretto. I live in India in a cosmopolitan city called Pune, mini-Oxford of India. I am a certified Life/Relationship Coach. I have done my post-graduation in psychology counselling. I have been married for 32 years with three grown-up children and a Restaurateur husband. I have seen the different shades of marriage and have given myself to my children's upbringing. I have enjoyed my journey in the various roles I have played as a wife, mother, daughter-in-law, sibling etc.

My journey made me realize my true purpose in life. I am equipped with the knowledge and self-realization to move ahead in life. Yes, my life has been a roller coaster ride with many lessons taught and learned. Unless you walk the path, you cannot reach your destination. No one can walk for you but can only show you the light to cross the dark alley in your life.

As a teenager, I worked in an NGO that cared for orphaned children and destitute women. I helped children in their daily school studies and told them stories. It was a challenging game, as children come with their baggage and mental turmoil. My focus was to fill their life with little joy and laughter. I also dreamt of getting married to a handsome, fearless man who would love and protect me, and we would live happily-ever-after ever after. That is what we read in the "Mills & Boons" and fairy tales' books. But honestly, that remains in the books, and real life is entirely different. Now I believe life is what you make of it. Life is like a railway track that runs parallel, along with laughter; there are tears, happiness, sadness, birth, death, and so on...

I have given 32 years to fulfil the dreams of my loved ones. Now, I have reached a stage where I want to reach out to millions to find their long-lost dreams, reinvent their passion, and move ahead in life to fulfil them. So, are you ready to walk the path with me to make it a smooth one?

I have chosen this purpose to help women and youth who feel stuck in their mundane lives and have lost sight of their actual goals and passion. I want to guide them to reinvent themselves, go towards their forgotten dreams, and fulfil their mission in life. I have chosen life/relationship coaching as my path to reach out to many who are experiencing the obstacles that I have faced, to help them to break all the shackles that are stopping them from fulfilling their dream mission. Life is the meaning you give it. Different moulds are placed before you; now, it is your choice to select the moulds and shape your life. We must pass many tests in life, so let us face them boldly with a big smile. No one can make you happy unless you are happy with yourself first.

Never mind, life is still beautiful.

**Rosy Barretto**
**https://linktr.ee/rosybarretto22**

An initiative of Mental Resilience Mastery © 2022

## THE HUNTING QUESTION

### MY PURPOSE IN LIFE

**To help people live a life of happiness, peace and fulfilment by creating an empowered mindset.**

### THE HUNTING QUESTION

You would not believe this, but when you start growing up and reach a point in your life, you might come across this question: "What is the real purpose of my life?"

Some may be dealing with existential crises, which could be good because our lives move in an autopilot mode where we are not even aware of who we are since we are running after the things that might please others or may bc trying to become like someone else, which our surroundings and people have approved. Interestingly, during this phase of life, we do not realise why we are doing what we are doing. One of the reasons that we can attribute this is that we are not living our lives with an intention. Our lives are just erratic, so people start feeling annoyed and disappointed. During this time, people will have conflicts and disagreements with their family members, spouse, friends, and office colleagues. The primary cause is that they are not synchronised with the source. The rhythm is missing.

## ABOUT ME

My name is Surbhi Pandey. I love to explore life the way it is. I have the most beautiful parents, and I live in Noida. I have worked as an actor in television series and short films and as an associate director. I am also a Kathak dancer and a voice-over artist who has given voice to several big platforms, series, movies, and documentaries. I am also a digital creator. I am now an author, an empowerment coach, and a certified yoga trainer.

I had a complete 360-degree change in my life that made me realise my purpose: to help people live a life of inner joy with an open and empowered mindset of huge possibilities to become happy and live a fulfilling life from within. It is not limited; it will expand as I move through this lovely life journey. I want to serve and contribute to the well-being of the people around me because people need that. There is already an ocean of pain and suffering, and I want this world to be the land of love, compassion, and happiness.

I remember being in the worst phase of my life, not just once but many times. When I was growing up, I never knew that positivity ever existed. Later on, during my journey at a young age, I discovered several aspects that brought me closer to examining and exploring life just the way it is.

I was in Mumbai, struggling to build a career in acting. I had landed good roles. I was the main lead actress in one of the daily television series on National Channel for almost 130 episodes. Somehow, things changed. My interest and motivation to build a career decreased to their lowest levels, leading to many ups and downs in my life. Mainly I had relationship issues, and that was draining.

I remember staying in bed, depressed and sulking all day, staring at the blank ceiling for hours, with no motivation to get out and do something. I was in and out of the kitchen, intending to end my life with a kitchen knife. Thankfully, I did not do that. The global virus pandemic, COVID-19, hit.

I decided to leave Mumbai and moved back to Noida, Delhi-NCR, with my parents. With regular counselling and the support of my parents, I regained my strength and started feeling better. But the ordeal was not over yet. I faced another horrendous experience in my life during which I was again broken, shaken, torn apart, and harassed, but I met it well. The moment I did it, it made me feel empowered and confident.

And now, every day, I feel so grateful and blessed to be able to breathe and experience a new moment in my life. My heart is filled with gratitude because I understand the value of life and its purpose: to keep going, exploring, learning, and discovering more about myself and the divine energy. These experiences taught me much about life; I am a much stronger person now.

I want to help people because they have no idea how limitless their potential is until they discover it. The truth is that we can create our own life and change it.

Whether we want to be wounded or become wise, the choice is in our hands.
Each person perceives situations differently. A person can look at a number from one direction and say it is 6, and the other person, from another direction, can say 9. Both are right in their way. It is just how they look at it.

We can wander around the world without any purpose or have a sense in our lives, move towards it, and discover who we are through those experiences.

## KNOWING YOUR PURPOSE; THE WHY

What is the tangible outcome of having a purpose in our lives, and why is it so important?

If we ask ourselves these questions, we will be inspired to wake up in the morning with drive and determination. Having a purpose in life gives you a direction because many people who do not have that clarity end up wasting their time or ending their lives. It is essential for all of us. It will undoubtedly be painful at times, but the person you will become on your journey through life will be phenomenal.

Why am I saying this? I never had a reason. Many people kept saying that it is essential to know your why. You know, sometimes we are so ignorant of the most crucial things in life that we create an illusion that we know everything. But that is not the truth. When you discover the "why" behind what you want to be and do in life, this "why" keeps you going and becomes an entirely different person.

When you have a reason to wake up in the morning, you will not need an alarm. Remember our school days? When the school organised a picnic, and we were supposed to arrive at 6:30 am, we arrived at 6 am. Why? Because we were excited about something new, and that is essential. But the question is, why can we not do it every single day?

## MY REALISATION

I chose to do it the day I realised I had got to do it. That day, I had a compelling reason to live my life and never give up. During this beautiful journey of life, I have been a channel through which I have helped many people. It is all due to God's grace. I sincerely pray to God to make me a medium through which I can spread love, happiness, and peace around me. We are all energies.

It is not just motivation but a genuine intention and connection with life's source and soul purpose. All we need to do is to tap into the limitless power of abundance around us. Sometimes it can be painful and make you feel exhausted, but it is just the moment we have to realise that it is trying to teach us something new about ourselves.

Interestingly, when you start looking from this perspective, you will be even more grateful for everything because it makes you better. You will have an open mindset to discover something interesting every day.

## PURPOSE THE DRIVER

Our intention and purpose drive us in our life because that gives us a sense of calmness, balance, focus, and direction. All we need to have within ourselves is faith and absolutely zero expectations. When we truly love who we are and what we do, we enjoy the process, which is more important than anything else.

For instance, I love to document things and create videos. I have programs on building strong mindsets and habits that will transform and help people. The girl who thought she could never do it did it. So, you, too, can.

**Surbhi Pandey:**
https://linktr.ee/surabhie

## LIFE IS MY MENTOR

My purpose in life is straightforward, to be happy and make people around me live happily. This life is not just for surviving but about spreading love and joy with all the people I know and meet. It is about making a difference by helping people in need.

I come from a middle-class family; my dad was a section officer in one of the Cigarette Manufacturing companies in Hyderabad, India. My mother is a housewife; I have two siblings, a brother and a sister. Life was going smooth; I was 17years old and enjoying my college life. One day a storm entered my life, and it shook my world; I lost my father; he was 45 years at the time when he passed away.

All responsibilities were on my shoulders as I was the eldest son. My mother was not that educated as she was confined to the duties of looking after children without any exposure to the outer world. She lost her partner very young and even went into depression. For more than 15 years, she has been on medication for depression. My education was not completed due to circumstances when my dad passed away. It was very tough to find a job for me without proper educational qualifications.

My family's financial condition was terrible; therefore, I had to take on different odd jobs while continuing my studies. And moving forward in life. At this point, my purpose in life was to fulfil my family responsibilities, that was my only moto, and I was successful in fulfilling the duties of my brother and sister's education and settling them in their career. I got married to the love of my life. And with the help of my wife, I have completed all my responsibilities, like my siblings, marriages. I mean that life has taught me many hard lessons, but I grew more robust and determined by each one. I could only enter the Marketing and Sales Profession with no proper academic background. I prospered in life. I sold everything on the planet. I then joined the corporate world and worked in that environment for over two decades.

I received recognition early in my professional journey; I was a PAN India top performer in Business Development among 100 branches all over India for one year. The company rewarded all the top performers with a vacation abroad. I had been given many

opportunities to attend international conferences; I was fortunate to visit countries like Hongkong, Malaysia, and Thailand. My earnings were outstanding, and all my responsibilities towards my family were fulfilled. Due to Professional politics and due to my excessive travelling, health issues arose. I took a break then I started my own business. After some time, I lost money and my business due to a lack of good experience in the industry. I returned to the corporate world. I was disappointed with myself because I was not successful in business and was not happy working for others; I went into a zone you can call depression. I was not as active or interested as earlier in earning money. I became a consultant for banking products, and I was not doing that great in my financial area. I was not happy with myself. Even though after being happily married to a beautiful person, we were not blessed with children, that was God's decision, and I always asked myself what next. Having fulfilled my family responsibilities, the question that kept coming to my mind was, what is my life's purpose? This is the question I ask God every day in my prayers. When the Pandemic entered the world, everyone's life was affected, and we experienced a total shutdown. Life was horrifying and terrible; nobody knew what would happen next. If you look at the positive side, the world has become a global village. With the help of technology, we could connect with everyone whenever we wanted to virtually, sitting at home. We could learn and interact with anyone from any part of the world. At this point, I came across a beautiful program of self-transformation and how to help others help themselves transform. I realize that my question to the Universe, what is the purpose of my life, is answered. God has given me a bigger mission to not only fulfil my family responsibilities; it is time now to take responsibility, to transform and impact other people's life. To contribute and help them to achieve their desired dreams.

I do not want anyone to experience or get stuck in a similar situation in life which I was in. So, my purpose in life is to be a better version of myself, that is, to be a better human being. Every day I want to see a better understanding of myself, using whatever life has taught me to grow personally and professionally. Nature has supported me by sending its help through various means on numerous occasions in the form of Avengers, who are human beings. Now my focus is to give back to society and contribute whatever I can. The knowledge and experience that life has given to me. I want to share to empower others. I want to be a lifelong learner and give back the same learning to society, and I just want to see happiness in people all around me. I want to give, give, give whatever I have in whatever form I can, in whatever possible way. To be a better

human being, a better version of myself, and to leave a legacy by setting an example in my life.
Thank you

**MV RAO.**

An initiative of Mental Resilience Mastery © 2022

## EMOTIONAL & PHYSICAL HEALTH AS

## MY PURPOSE

"The purpose of life is not to be happy. It is to be useful, to be honourable, to be compassionate, to have it make some difference that you have lived and lived well."
**-RALPH WALDO EMERSON**

**MYBIO**

I am **Nutan Nakra** from India. I am an Emotional, Physical and Spiritual Wellness Action Coach, Counsellor, and Trainer. I am a qualified and trained teacher from Delhi University, Hindu College, with a Master's degree in Biochemistry. I am a certified International Coach. I am an author of an upcoming book on Health and Happiness. I come from a very modest, decent and hardworking family where my parents spent all their youth working extremely hard to give their three children the best life they could. I followed in their footsteps and shared the same with my family and children. A time came when I realized that I had gotten free from most of my essential responsibilities and duties, and the children had moved on in search of a better life for themselves.

My life had become quite empty and slow, with little excitement each day. I started finding life aimless with no progress. I started killing time in aimless activities like shopping uselessly. I forced visits to known and unknowns, which led to unnecessary expenses and the feeling of worthlessness and frustration. I was lucky to find a book named IKIGAI and realized that I need to seriously work on my life purpose, which should be such that it may give me excited to wake up each morning. It should be so satisfying that I may never get tired of doing it. I may go out of my way fulfilling that purpose and still not mind it. This will ultimately give me happiness, satisfaction, progressiveness, worthiness, and respect in my own eyes. After searching for days and months and observing where I liked to spend most of my time, I decided to work on the emotional and physical well-being of the people around me. I had always worked on deep emotional levels to dig out why people fell sick again and again without any visible outside reasons. I realized that people have Anxiety, Stress, Fears, Doubts, Anger, Revenge fullness, Dissatisfaction, etc. All kinds of negative emotions have a damaging effect on our nervous system. They weaken our body and Immune system. Such stressful situations stimulate our Endocrine System, and as a result, stress hormones start flowing in every cell; this results in symptoms like trembling, uneven breathing, sweating, irregular heartbeat, heart palpitation, rise in blood pressure, fainting, chest pain, stomach upset and depression.

Since health and happiness were my favourite subjects and I had been reading and researching about them all my life, I started studying in-depth about them. I joined an organization with the tools, techniques, and skills to work on the diseases people suffer from. They worked on the subject so that people may become healthy, more energetic, and more productive and hence could lead healthy, happy, and longer life. Today I have a mission to bring health and longevity to society. For this aim, I have created a mastermind group of people with the vision to Live Long and Live Young. My dream now is to create happy, healthy and ever-young Super Humans. I have developed programs and workshops which help people.

1. Overcome their old doubts and fears and improve their inner power and self-esteem.
2. To create appropriate balance in domestic and professional life.
3. Learn to live a life of healthy discipline to gain progressiveness.
4. Learn to establish respectful and caring relationships among the organization's members, friends, and relatives.

This platform allowed me to interact with people far away from my close social circle. I realized that people suffer from self-created fears, doubts, and inhibitions, which give them an inferiority complex. Women and young children were emotionally suppressed and abused, and they lacked courage and self-respect. This adversely affected their health, happiness, and progressiveness. I have created an online and offline club where we all interact regularly and work on emotional and physical problems to bring good health and happiness to their lives. Since I started doing this, I have gotten a spark back in my life. I love to share the knowledge I gathered all my life which brings happiness, productivity filled with excellent health, and long life. People show colossal love and gratitude towards me, which has made my life very satisfying, with a burning desire to live. My purpose today gives me a significant driving force, and I am quickly finding the path to reach them. I have pledged to contribute to the lives of the poor by uplifting them and giving them relevant knowledge and support systems.

Many women have found their purpose in my field of work, and today I am part of a massive community with common goals. My job gives me Buzz moments, due to which I like to spend my money, energy, and time unconditionally. My life parameters related to relationships, progressiveness, spirituality, growth, carrier, and money have improved many folds. I never get bored in my life, and genuine well-wishers constantly surround me. Today I have found my purpose in life and formed means to execute it and have people around me who help me fulfil my life dreams. I have started respecting my capabilities and strengths, and they have become my best friend. I have disciplined my life to wake up early morning before sunrise and go for a 45 to 50 minutes' walk. I have learned the importance of my Me Time to improve my creativity and learn to relax. I have developed a meditation habit to strengthen my inner self and bring natural recharging of my mind. I have grown close-knit genuine relationships in my community as strong life anchors. I have learned to filter my thoughts and allow only the progressive, positive ones to enter, which fills me with excitement, energy, and happiness. I have learned to distance myself from toxic and harmful situations and people to avoid any negativity in my life. Today I have a mission to reach out to at least ten new people every day and educate them, train them and habituate them to take charge of their emotional, physical, and spiritual well-being and craft progressive goals for their life on a monthly and yearly manner so that they may build life coping skills, improve social skills and become emotionally and financially independent. To fulfil this mission of my life, I have joined the Centre for children with special needs in Khanpur, Delhi, to meet the Emotional needs of children aged 15 to 20. I visit various Educational Institutes and look after the needs of these children. I have been a member of the Inner Wheel Club of India for the last 11 years, and I hold workshops for women in the age group of 25 to 60 years. I am an active member of Rotary Club International, and I do projects for people for the cancer society and nursing home. Today's life has a new spark filled with happiness, satisfaction, and ever-growing pleasure. I have naturally become empathetic, compassionate, warmhearted, cheerful, and thoughtful. I have become a great listener and always love to volunteer for good causes. I get along very well with people in general very quickly. I naturally look for the good in everyone. This is a significant character shift I have developed. I highly recommend everyone to experience this valuable lifestyle gift from me.

**Nukan Nakra:**
https://linktr.ee/nutannakra

An initiative of Mental Resilience Mastery © 2022

# SPIRIT OF NEVER GETTING

# DEFEATED IN LIFE

Everybody undergoes challenges in life. I, too, experienced innumerable challenges but overcame everything, and now I am a winner in life. I am a single woman, yet very strong. My purpose in life now is to make other single women robust, confident and happy.

I am Kala Natrajan, an ex-banker. I am now the published solo author of 3 books, a co-author of 5 books, a life transformation coach and a motivational speaker. I love helping people, empowering them and giving them breakthroughs.
I am well educated and have done my M.Com., CAIIB, Diploma in treasury, investment and Risk management and MBA in finance.

I am a philanthropist and am particularly interested in social work and helping the poor and underprivileged.

My life is an inspiration to others. I faced multiple challenges in life yet paved a path for other women to follow. From a person who was herself under-confident, I am now helping others build their confidence and self-worth.

As a single woman, you may be separated or divorced or widowed. You could also be unmarried. I understand that the onus is on you to fend for yourself and your children. Not only this, you have to earn enough money for the child's education and professional courses, which nowadays cost a fortune. The main thing is taking charge of your life. I want to work towards building a bright future for them. There are several issues which single women face, and their doubts and complaints are innumerable. I want them to create their own identity in life, earn money and be respected in society. Last but not least, I want them to be happy and at peace. This is my dream now.

I was born into a middle-class family. My family consisted of my maternal grandfather, my parents and my three elder sisters. My three sisters and I had an age gap of 12 years, ten years and 5-1/2 years. My eldest sister dominated so much over me that I was scared, shy, timid and meek. In my school, I was a good student and won many prizes in elocution, including the inter-school elocution competition. Even when I was a child, I had to do most of my things independently as both my parents worked full time. My mother was working as a matron in an orphanage, and we were given quarters to stay inside the orphanage. Since we were living inside the orphanage, I befriended the girl inmates of the orphanage, and they were big bullies. When I was ten years of age, I complained to my two elder sisters about the girls bullying me, and my eldest sister said I was a big girl now. I must handle my life on my own. I should not go to her and complain like a child. So, I completely stopped telling my problems at home. As a child, I wore so shabbily dressed to school as there was no one to take care of me. When I was in 7th grade, my scalp was full of scabies which was very painful.

In 9th grade, I won 4 prizes in an elocution competition and became very popular in school. Other students in my class became extremely jealous of me. When I went to 10th grade at the age of 13 years+, the school uniform at that time was a white cotton saree and white blouse. On the first day of school, I was given the old saree and blouse that belonged to my elder sister, and since there was no one in the house to help me with it, I had to wear the saree on my own. I didn't know how to wear the saree and just rolled it over the dress and went to school. I must have looked like an urchin, and the students, especially boys and 2-3 girls, started playing cheap tricks on me and calling me names. As days passed, the ragging became more severe, and I was deeply offended. Once, they hung a calendar in the classroom of a girl wearing skimpy clothes and said it was me. All this started making a profound negative impact on my mind, and I became a nervous wreck. Although struggling with my concentration, I somehow passed my secondary school certificate examination in 1st class and got admission to a prestigious commerce college.

When I went to college, I was extremely shy, timid, meek, with no self-esteem and very scared of boys. I had no concentration, obsessive thoughts, and imagination but kept passing my exams until 1st year of BCom. When I went to the final year of BCom, I was petrified of everything and scared to death. I kept getting destructive thoughts about myself and could not appear for my exams. Nobody at home knew about my situation; everybody became angry and stopped talking to me. Next year I appeared for my final BCom exams, and I passed. My mental condition was so bad that I shut myself off from the world and contemplated taking my own life. I decided I would jump into the sea or drink poison. Somehow, I got the courage to live and started working. My colleagues also started ragging me since I was so timid and scared.

As if this was not enough, I got married, which was traumatic. When my husband started physically abusing me, I walked out of the marriage and eventually took a divorce. My father passed away in 2004, and my mother in 2006, leaving me all alone in this world. I got a killer's instinct in me that I would win in life no matter what and make my mother proud of me. I took a strong determination that I would do all that it takes and work hard consistently towards achieving my dreams.

When I was about to be divorced, I had lots of fears in my mind.
What will the world think of me?
What will my colleagues say?
What will my relatives say?
Will others respect me and many more?
then, I was determined to make the best out of my life. I focussed on my self-growth and became self-confident.

It's not about what the world thinks about you but about what you feel about yourself that matters. The whole world can be on one side, yet you must stand up for yourself. Nothing else matters if you think you are right and on the right track. The day you stop respecting yourself, everyone will stop doing the same.

It's all in my mind. When you change your mindset, everything else changes. No situation in life is good or bad. It's your attitude that determines everything.

When you change your perspective to win, everything will reorient towards your success.

A great philosopher has said that you must never get defeated by failures and try again and again until you succeed.

Today I can call myself a winner in life. However, it took a lot of effort on my part. Since I suffered so much, my purpose now is to empower single women to stand tall in life and achieve success.

I am now a published author of 3 books - 'empower yourself', 'reinvent yourself' and 'born to fight.

My vision is to make 100 single women strong so that they stand up on their own feet.

An initiative of Mental Resilience Mastery © 2022

As an empowerment coach for single women and a motivational speaker, I aim to empower single women, making India a better place to live in.

**Kala Natrajan:**

**https://linktr.ee/kalathegreat.**

# PERSEVERANCE

My life's purpose is to empower the mindset of Children, parents, and individuals. To motivate them to live happy and successful life.

## Mission
My mission is to provide clarity to my clients by listening, encouraging, inspiring, and motivating them to excel in all aspects of their life. I provide customized strategies so that they can achieve their outcomes within a given time.

## Vision
My vision is to enable my clients to identify their goals accordingly to their talents and aid them in overcoming the challenges they may be facing. My dream is to provide customized tools and strategies to achieve their goals. Proper mindset coaching will provide my clients with the necessary tools and skills to succeed and help them see the world through a more positive lens.

## My Story

An initiative of Mental Resilience Mastery © 2022

I have always believed in making your dreams come true; even as a little girl, my dreams were more significant than anyone could ever think. I was fortunate to be brought up in a family where both my parents were highly inspiring and motivating; that being said, my life came with its challenges. We moved around countless times, which caused me to change schools' multiple times, and I had to re-adjust to various new environments. To alleviate
the burden of these transition periods, I joined numerous clubs, activities, and even sports, and involving myself in these activities allowed me to make friends fast. I participated in tournaments, meets, and competitions in these clubs, often winning prizes while representing my school.

Upon finishing school, I was destined to pursue my love for finance, hoping to work in the banking field. During university, I was not only an excellent student but also aimed to help people. One of the ways I achieved this was by setting up university-wide events and activities for everyone to participate in. Eventually, after lots of hard work and perseverance, I got my first job at Peerless® and finally found my way into Standard Chartered®. Standard Chartered was and still is one of the biggest banks in the world, and my hard work paid off as I succeeded in achieving my goal of working in a bank. I went on to work at a couple of different institutions, from banks to managing small firms. My bachelor's and MBA paid off due to my ambitious goals and allowed me to be a successful female in a country where women are looked down upon.

Soon after my family and I moved to Saudi Arabia, I realized the importance of preschool for toddlers. I, along with many scientific reports, believe that 80% of a child's brain development occurs before seven. Being a parent myself, experiencing my two boys' development, and understanding everything they went through, I decided to start my preschool. After tons of reading and learning about a young child's brain functions and how they develop and grow, in 2016, my preschool welcomed its first student and future pioneers.

**Aiding Individuals**
Being a parent, I understand parental expectations. I support parents in providing the right learning environment for their children at home. Because I believe in my message, I also decided to write a book called: "How preschool can change your kids' life," which is now available on Amazon. This book is aimed

at adults, so they will understand everything I learned through years of experience in social work, parenting two kids, and my work experience.

With my vast experience in corporate banking and management and as an educator, I am confident I can help children, parents, and individuals to live their dream life. With my desire to make a difference in people's lives, I decided to help more people than just toddlers. I decided that life coaching would be the perfect way to do so. From there on, I have become a certified life coach by the International Coaching Federation (ICF) certified program and have done countless workshops and programs.

I believe that "All winners are lifelong learners," and I have implemented this in my life. From the day I was born till now, I have never stopped learning, regardless of my other goals. Even working in the corporate world, I continued my education. And throughout opening my preschool to becoming a certified life coach, I have continued learning consistently about countless different topics.

Everyone has unique core values, knowledge, and talents, which will help them grow. The mindset of the individuals is shaped according to their genetics, upbringing, and different kind of experiences in their life. As a life coach, I aim to highlight these characteristics of a person and aid them throughout the process of applying their curated knowledge and talents to become the best version of themselves. My coaching strategy aims to support my clients through customized development paths and to motivate and support them in unleashing their full potential. To lead a happy and successful life, the individual should feel comfortable and satisfied in all areas of life.

As a woman, I can understand the challenges we face throughout different stages in our life, on both personal and professional fronts. I feel that every female should take charge of their life so that they can achieve anything they desire. We women do not have to be dependent on anyone for anything; we can all be independent and successful. We, women, are powerful and more than capable of becoming successful, financially independent, and being the best version of ourselves.

Recently I have spoken at numerous events hosted by NGOs and workshops, and I had the pleasure of starting my workshop called "Uplift Your Mood", which I host weekly on zoom. I aim to continue speaking at such events to influence and motivate as many people as I can reach. Along with these workshops, I have my own goals to help people, such as the homeless population or orphans; instead of opening a homeless shelter or orphanage, I want to innovate and solve the problem on a larger scale.

**Asha Bharti**
Educator, Author
Empowering Mindset Coach (Children, Parents, and Individuals)
An initiative of Mental Resilience Mastery © 2022

Connect with me
**https://linktr.ee/coach_asha**:

"Recently I came across a book called " The Grail" by David Nair and a few of the persons he has been guiding in coaching and Presentation skills.

The authors have written recounting their journey in self-development to enable others to undertake similar efforts in self-development by vicarious experiencing the stages in moving forward.

The book could be handy for persons in the helping professions of Training, Social development, social work as it will enable them to give direction to their efforts in self-development."

-Aarush Joshi

"There is that Philosophy in life which I tremendously believe in, that is " I CAN'T GIVE SOMETHING WHICH I DONT HAVE". It is and will always be the immediate intention of a coach to deliver the message of hope, to declare what the world needs, and recreate paths for people at their losing ends.

The book will allow you to realize you are never alone, you got a fantastic team, and you got YOU! Don't you ever forget that! How do you do it? Well, simply breathe, hear your surroundings, release your breathwork, and you will realize, magnify and magnetize what your heart is looking for. It seeks you intensely as you embrace the authors and hear their stories by simply using your heart! One at a time, page by page, patience and kindness. When you experience this transition and belief can emoti9nally alter your life, not tomorrow but right NOW; that means PURPOSE must be sought wholeheartedly by allowing these excellent writers to show who they are and how they get to where they are at. Never forget to refill your empty cup, eat read, listen. You will tremendously know your meaning in life and listen through your heart."

- Coach Vee Lee

An initiative of Mental Resilience Mastery © 2022

# EPILOGUE

Grail – Tick your Life Right, with Purpose, was born after working 25 years with over 250,000 people from various countries and cultures, backgrounds, professions, and echelons in the community. Through my course of the journey of developing people, I found many lacked one crucial ingredient in their lives - Definite Major Purpose.

People have goals and aspirations, and they achieve them. Despite completing their projects, they were still left high and dry, with a feeling of a void within themselves, not being satisfied, basically Self Actualized, on account of lack of fulfilment.

This "slack of" internal fortitude, the internal bliss, contentment, and the want and need to contribute from a higher plane created internal conflict, internal disarray, frustration, and sometimes depression. Admittedly they are making money but were they Happy?

**"The Purpose of our Life is to be Happy."**
-Dalai Lama

This prompted me to pull together a mastermind called Mental Resilience Mastery and work with 50 members from across four continents. In building the mental and physical resilience, skilling them up, and while doing so, stretch them further by seeding the idea of - "what if" we wrote a book titled Purpose, elaborating on how we arrived at each of our purposes and how it would help us attain self-actualisation.

This snowballed to us Self-Publishing, marketing distribution, and the arrangements to donate the proceeds to a charity in India. That was the journey so far.

What does the future hold for these purpose-driven Members?

An initiative of Mental Resilience Mastery © 2022

They are developing their programs, workshops, and public speaking gigs. Whilst that is under their belt, they will pay it forward by guiding the next batch of MRM members to search for their purpose and write the second book on the subject with the subsequent assemblage. This will be done in an ongoing way. The intent is to create a dint within the community to roll out such best practices.

I am eternally grateful to the team that helped pull this together, mainly my right-hand person Dr Sumana Chakraborty who gave unconditionally and drove the team to meet set deadlines and the Team leaders who pulled their socks to complete their side of the projects.

This collective pull was not easy. It is on the same page with a dedicated team driven to have 'Grail' as a New York Times Best Seller is the burning desire of the group. This is going the group even further.

Your support in purchasing a copy and circulating the message for others to do the same would be most appreciated. All proceeds from the sales of the book are going to an NGO.

David Nair
https://linktr.ee/DavidNair
An initiative of Mental Resilience Mastery © 2022

# INFLUENCERS OPINION ON GRAIL

"This book provides an SPC formula to readers Strength, Passion, Clarity- which will help them to develop and sustain a PURPOSE…"

**Walter Vieira**

"If I were to imagine a book that called out to me, it would surely be GRAIL..".

**Suresh Mansharmani**

"This book examines thirty global influencers pursuit of life's meaning. Strongness, passion, and clarity are just a few of the subthemes that can be explored by the reader…"

**Dr Sandeep Chalke**

"A life without a purpose is a listless journey where a human being is reduced to a dried autumn leaf, spinelessly blowing in the wind. Purpose in life drives us to achieve our goals and helps us find happiness through achievements…
"**Ralph de Sousa**

"The book will allow you to realize you are never alone, you got a fantastic team, and you got YOU!"

**Coach Vee Lee**

An initiative of Mental Resilience Mastery © 2022

"The book could be handy for persons to give direction to their efforts in exploring possibilities of self-development..."

**Aarush Joshi**